Record Breaker!

With twenty seconds remaining, Jefferson High's star center Brian Davis needed only four more points to break the team record.

Guard Reggie Dupree led Brian with a long pass that he caught while racing toward the basket. With his teammates behind him, Brian turned and scored the lay-up.

Two points to go.

"Press 'em!" Coach Williams shouted.

The Truman High forward arrived to inbound the ball, but stalled for time as the seconds ticked away. Brian saw that Truman's only open player was their reserve center thirty feet from the basket. Just as the forward fired the pass, Brian leaped and intercepted it.

In one fluid motion, Brian turned and lofted a thirty-foot shot. The buzzer sounded as the ball floated toward the hoop, nudged against the backboard, and dropped back down through the cords!

Other books in the **HOOPS** series:

#1: Fast Breaks

HOOPS

LONG-SHOT
CENTER

Kirk Marshall

BALLANTINE BOOKS • NEW YORK

Special thanks to Steve Clark.

RLI: VL: 6 & up
      ———————
      IL: 6 & up

Produced by the Jeffrey Weiss Group, Inc.
133 Fifth Avenue
New York, New York 10003

Library of Congress Catalog Card number: 88-92813

ISBN 0-345-35909-7

Manufactured in the United States of America

First Edition: June 1989

For the fine people of Indianapolis,
especially Chris, Herb,
and my other friends at Butler University.

ONE

Brian Davis, the six-foot-eight-inch starting center for the Jefferson High Patriots, passed his
basketball behind his back and to his other
hand with the ease and skill of an experienced
playmaker. Hoping to complete the fancy
Harlem Globetrotter-type routine he had practiced in the privacy of his bedroom, he then
tried to spin the orange ball on his right index
finger for as long as he could.

But before he could balance the basketball, it
slipped off his finger and bounced into the
narrow street in one of Indianapolis's poorest
inner-city neighborhoods, barely missing a passing car. Jefferson teammates Reggie Dupree and
Tony Zarella, who were walking alongside Brian
and spinning their own basketballs, laughed and
shook their heads.

"Man, you'll never be a Globetrotter that way," Reggie said to Brian. The five-foot-ten-inch black guard elbowed Tony playfully, then added, "Maybe our boy needs a training ball."

Tony, a short and stocky white guard with bushy black hair and some shadowy stubble on his face, laughed. "Yeah, how about a ball with training wheels to keep it on his finger?" Brian's two best friends since he moved to the big city six months ago high-fived each other.

Brian pulled the collar of his parka up against the cold December breeze, then hustled after his ball. Each member of the Jefferson High varsity was given a new basketball and was supposed to carry it wherever he went.

Just before Brian caught up with the rolling ball, it smashed into several battered trash cans on the opposite sidewalk, upending them. A lid rolled a few feet away and fell onto its side with a loud metallic crash.

Brian froze in his tracks and looked around at the rundown neighborhood, twenty blocks from the city's main business district. Hoping he hadn't disturbed anyone, he glanced at the nearby redbrick tenements and the small dilapidated wood-frame houses farther down the street. Several pawnshops and liquor stores, their windows covered with heavy metal screens, completed the scene before him.

The cold December wind moaned through a nearby alley, kicking up dust and candy wrappers and other pieces of debris into small tornadoes that spun toward Brian, causing him to squint. He pulled his parka tighter as icy fingers of wintry air probed the cracks and creases of his clothing, making him shiver.

"Come on, Davis," he heard Tony yelling from across the street.

"Yeah, man," Reggie added. "We're going to be late unless you get moving. Besides, we're freezing our butts off over here."

As Brian bent over to grasp his basketball, he noticed an elderly black woman staring at him from behind a first-floor window of the apartment building in front of him. Her eyes made Brian uncomfortable.

At the same moment, a small group of young men, mostly black, but including a couple of white guys, peered at him from the entrance of another apartment building half a block away. Several of them were holding half-empty wine bottles. The expressions on their faces were hard and mean, and Brian suddenly wished he hadn't been so clumsy while performing his Globetrotter routine.

Brian picked up his ball and walked briskly across the street to where Reggie and Tony were waiting for him. "Let's go," he said, shivering and holding his basketball under his arm this time. His breath was steamy in the cold air.

"Man, it's about time," Reggie said, pulling his wool knit cap farther down over his nearly shaven head. "We figured you were trying to make some new friends or something."

"No way. This neighborhood gives me the creeps. Last summer when we played basketball games down here, it wasn't too bad, but now it's the pits." He looked at Reggie. "How much farther to the community center?"

"About four more blocks."

"You're lucky we decided to come along and keep an eye on you, Davis," Tony said, also spinning his ball with ease. "I really should be back in my warm living room watching the Pacers and Bulls game on TV."

"But don't worry, man," Reggie added, still spinning his ball. "Tony and me'll protect our homeboy from all the bad dudes down here in the big city."

Reggie and Tony laughed and high-fived each other, and the three of them walked hunched over into the teeth of a stiff breeze.

For Brian, the last six months or so had seen some big changes in his life. On July fourth he and his mother had moved from the small farm town of Paintville, Indiana, to the state's capital, Indianapolis. The move followed the separation of his parents because of his dad's heavy drinking, and Brian and his mom had moved into his Aunt Margaret's two-story wood-frame house in a crowded neighborhood on the city's northeast side.

Brian, at six eight and with a feathery touch on his long jump shots, had been one of Indiana's top high school basketball players at Paintville High. In fact, he had been named to the third-team all-state all-star team after his sophomore season.

Following his move to Indianapolis, he spent the summer learning the rough inner-city style of play before beginning his junior year at

Jefferson High School. He became friends with Reggie and Tony, then most of the other basketball players. And after some early concerns about adjusting to the big city, he finally felt at ease in the rather run-down inner-city high school—especially once basketball season began.

For Brian and his Jefferson High teammates, led by young head coach Tom Ford, the season began successfully with two close victories. Brian had adjusted well to the faster style of play found in the city. His accurate outside shooting had helped him score fifteen and twenty points in their first two games during the last week of November.

But when the Jefferson High varsity traveled to Terre Haute, Indiana, for a four-team tournament, Brian and his teammates learned they needed to work even harder on their game. In the tourney's opening game, they were trounced 85–70 by highly regarded Gary Tech, a large school from northern Indiana.

And despite Jefferson's victory in the consolation game against a small Clayville team, Brian and his coaches realized that he needed to develop some offensive moves to the basket. The added threat of some quick moves would keep their larger and better opponents from playing up close to Brian, to prevent him from taking his deadly outside jump shots.

Mel Williams, the team's assistant coach, arranged for Brian to begin some informal one-on-one work on offensive basketball moves later in the afternoon with Tyrone Russell, a tall

black former star at Jefferson. The site was to
be a small community recreation center in the
middle of the city's toughest neighborhood
where Tyrone lived.

Now Brian, tired but determined to become
the best basketball player he could possibly be,
forced himself to forget about the unfriendly
surroundings of the downtown neighborhood
and trudged along the windy sidewalk. The
three of them turned a corner, and Brian was
grateful that a building was now blunting the
full force of the icy breeze.

"What do you guys know about this Tyrone
Russell?" he asked, blowing on his hands to
warm them.

Reggie bounced his basketball a few times on
the sidewalk, then looked up at Brian. "The
dude was a great player at Jefferson five years
ago. Some say he's the best that ever played
there. Man, he's got the moves."

"Reggie's right," Tony added, pulling the collar of his coat up around his stubbled face. "I've
seen him play a few times during summer ball.
He's the best playground player ever in the city.
There's nobody who can stop him. But it's too
bad about his problems at college."

Brian kept walking alongside his friend.
"What happened?" he asked.

"Tyrone got in with a bad crowd," Reggie said.
"You know, coke and everything, even though
Tyrone doesn't do drugs. He's too smart for that.
But it was one of those colleges with not too
much for the black brothers to do socially, you
know, except drive around town looking for

action. Tyrone should have picked another school."

"He could have, too," Tony said. "I remember reading in the paper that over two hundred colleges wanted Tyrone to play for them."

"So, anyway," Reggie continued, "Tyrone was a starter for this college's basketball team until he was caught by the police in the same car as these bad dudes. Tyrone was innocent, even the guys he was with told that to the cops. But his college didn't like the bad publicity or something and took away his basketball scholarship."

"Tyrone's two brothers both got in trouble here in Indianapolis with drugs and the police," Tony interjected. "So Tyrone tried to make something of himself, and look what happened."

Reggie continued. "Tyrone came back to Indianapolis and married his high school girl friend, but his big-time basketball days were over. They got a couple of kids now, but all Tyrone can do is work as a recreation leader at this community center we're heading for." Reggie paused and shook his head. "What a waste of basketball talent."

Brian glanced around him at the run-down buildings. "If he lives down here," he said, wondering how people could exist in such bad conditions, "I guess it's a wasted life, too."

Brian and his two friends continued along the sidewalk for another minute or so until they spotted two other Jefferson High teammates, their captain, LaMont Jackson, and his best friend, Clarence Reed. Both of the tall black

kids lived nearby, and now they were waiting
with basketballs in their hands for Brian to
begin his lessons with Tyrone. Behind them,
Brian noticed as he approached, was a broken-
down redbrick building with a sign over the
front entrance that read Maple Street Community and Recreation Center.

But as Brian, Reggie, and Tony reached their
two teammates, Brian noticed the grim expression on Clarence's usually happy face. Even
LaMont, who was known for keeping his cool in
most situations, seemed upset for some reason.

"What's up, dude?" Reggie asked, his breath
steamy in the cold air. "You seen Tyrone?"

Clarence shook his head. "Something bad's
going down over near Tyrone's place," said the
muscular six-foot-three-inch forward. Clarence
was wearing a pair of protective goggles he
used during games up on his head over his knit
cap. And like the others, including LaMont, he
was carrying his Jefferson basketball.

Brian turned his attention to LaMont, a wiry
six-foot-two forward, as he shuffled his feet
nervously and pointed with his thumb back at
the entrance to the community center.

"The old caretaker inside says police cars and
TV vans have been arriving around the block
for the past half hour," the Jefferson varsity captain said. In the six months Brian had known
LaMont he never had seen him so agitated. "The
old guy says it's a drug bust, and he thinks it's in
the apartment building where Tyrone lives with
his wife and kids."

Without wasting any more time, Brian and his

four Jefferson High teammates raced around the next corner and ran down a narrow street toward a five-story apartment building several blocks away. As he approached the building, Brian saw a dozen police cars parked near the front entrance, their rooftop lights still flashing. Two instacam television vans with their stations' call letters painted on their sides were also parked nearby.

"Yeah, that's Tyrone's place," Reggie said, panting, as they all stopped near a line of wooden police barricades fifty yards from the building's entrance. "Look at all the commotion around here."

Besides the television reporters and the police, a crowd of a hundred or so curious onlookers had gathered across the street from the five-story building. Most of the people were black and apparently lived nearby. Clarence and LaMont stepped quickly over to the crowd and talked to several people before they hustled back to Brian and the others with some news.

"It's a drug bust, all right," Clarence said, still trying to catch his breath. "Somebody tipped off the police, and now they're trying to flush out some dudes from the apartment building. Nobody knows who the police are after, or even if the dudes are really in there."

Suddenly two loud popping sounds, like gunshots, filled the cold afternoon air. Several women in the crowd cried out in surprise, and Brian turned toward the police cars just in time to see two tear-gas cannisters smash through a couple of the apartment building's second-story windows. A cloud of tear gas began pouring out of the broken windows.

"Man," Reggie said, wide-eyed, "it's just like TV."

Soon a stream of apartment building residents, choking on the gas and trying to wipe it from their eyes, began stumbling out through the front entrance. As Brian watched, half a dozen police officers with gas masks hurtled past the stunned residents and entered the building. A few minutes later, the officers returned with several white guys and two black men in handcuffs.

"Look," Tony shouted, pointing. "That last black guy in handcuffs. It's Tyrone!"

Brian was stunned at the news, and the five teammates stared intently. "You're right, man," Reggie said, "it's Tyrone, and it looks like he's in big trouble. Maybe we oughtta call Coach Williams. He lives pretty close to here."

Lamont and Clarence ran toward a nearby grocery store to make the phone call. Brian watched as the police put Tyrone Russell, the greatest basketball player in Jefferson High history, into the backseat of a police car.

TWO

While Brian and the others waited in the cold for Coach Williams to arrive, a young black woman and her two small children were escorted from the building by an officer. The woman and her kids walked to where Tyrone was sitting in the backseat of a police cruiser.

"That's Tyrone's wife and kids," Clarence said, shaking his head slowly. "It's too bad this happened to her. She's an all-right woman. Helps Tyrone work with the kids at the community center."

Several minutes later, Coach Williams drove up. The big black varsity assistant, a six-foot-five-inch former star center at Butler University twenty years before, strode briskly over to the group of players. As he approached, the broad-shouldered coach with a black-and-silver

11

goatee on his chin gazed at the police cars in front of the apartment building.

"Coach, it looks bad for Tyrone," Tony said.

Stroking his goatee, Coach Williams nodded a greeting to the players, then said in his deep baritone voice, "Wait here, guys, and let me find out what's happening." The heavyset coach then walked across the street toward the police cars.

"Man, this is unbelievable," Reggie said. The skinny black guard peered at the police cars, his face a mask of disbelief. "Tyrone's a real good dude."

Tony nodded. "Yeah, I remember when he even won some award from the mayor's office and was on the TV news. Believe it or not, it was for his antidrug work with the neighborhood kids down here."

"Hey, look," Clarence said, pointing at the police car, where Tyrone was getting out of the backseat. "They're taking off his handcuffs. It looks like he's been set free."

Then, to Brian's delight, Coach Williams helped Tyrone take his family back into the apartment building and led the former star player across the street. Reggie, Clarence, and LaMont rushed up to Tyrone and exchanged high-fives with him, and Brian heard a burst of Reggie's high-pitched laughter.

" It was all a case of mistaken identity," Coach Williams said in his deep voice. He smiled. "After the police put Tyrone in the back seat of the car, several officers recognized him as one of the city's top volunteers in the war against drugs. Even one of the drug dealers said Tyrone was innocent and had nothing to do with them."

Coach Williams introduced Tyrone to Brian, who shook his hand and felt his firm grip. The black six-six former star center was well built, with broad shoulders and long arms. His face was wide and fleshy and sort of mean-looking, but his friendly brown eyes and the broad grin parting his lips gave Brian a hint of his real nature.

"How you doing, man," Tyrone said, looking Brian up and down. "I've been looking forward all day to working with you."

"Same here."

Tyrone nodded and high-fived Brian.

Coach Williams smiled and slapped Tyrone on the back. "Well," the coach said, "you can head on over to the community center and show Davis here some of those moves to the basket you're so famous for. I got to be heading home now."

"Thanks, Coach," the boys said as the coach walked toward his car.

"Okay, man, let's go and see what this white boy's got." Tyrone smiled and led the way back along the darkening, windy city streets.

To Brian, the interior of the community center seemed as run-down as the outside. The narrow building's many small windows either were cracked or had holes in them covered with cardboard, and the basketball court was scarred and warped. The air inside was heavy with the stench of stale cigarettes, sweaty socks, and musty shower stalls. And when the old caretaker switched on the overhead lights, Brian barely noticed much difference in the dusky light inside the building.

Reggie looked at Brian and laughed. "Man, I bet you never saw a court like this down on the farm. In this kind of place, you learn how to play radar-ball 'cause of the bad light." He cackled again.

Brian and Tyrone took one end of the court for themselves, while Reggie and the other Jefferson players shot baskets at the other. Two dozen or so small black kids lined the narrow court and watched the action.

Handling his basketball with the confident ease of an accomplished shooter, Brian took shot after shot and swished almost all of them, while Tyrone rebounded for him. At one point, Brian swished twenty-five long jumpers in a row, causing the small kids to ooh and aah. His Jefferson teammates stopped their own shooting to watch the exhibition.

After ten minutes or so, Tyrone nodded his head and told Brian, "Brian, having such a great outside shot ought to make your drives to the basket easier. The defense'll probably play up close to stop your outside shot, and that'll leave you wide open for drives to the hoop."

Brian nodded. "That's what happened during our first four games, but I had trouble going to the basket."

"Well, I should be able to help you out," Tyrone said. "And it shouldn't take too long. Let me show you some basic moves first, then over the next couple of weeks or so we'll start the shake-and-bake stuff you see on the playground."

For the next ten minutes, Brian witnessed some of the fanciest offensive moves he had ever seen. Tyrone seemed to know more fakes and feints than Brian had even thought about. And as the big former all-star danced and whirled and dribbled his way to the basket, Brian noticed that Reggie, Tony, and the others had stopped their shooting around and were watching Tyrone's one-man exhibition.

Next, Tyrone gave Brian the ball and began to teach him the footwork involved in several of his more basic, but effective, moves to the hoop. Tyrone played defensive, and within a few minutes Brian was jab-stepping, leg-hooking, and using several other fancy moves to get free for a drive to the basket. He felt as if he were a new player, and in a way he was.

"Dy-no-mite," Reggie said, walking over to Brian and Tyrone.

"I can almost hear the other coaches groaning already," Tony added.

And for the next half hour, Brian, Tony, and LaMont played a half-court game against Tyrone, Clarence, and Reggie. The first team to reach twenty baskets was going to be the winner, and almost immediately Tony passed the ball in to Brian, who was being guarded by Tyrone. The former all-star seemed undecided about how close he wanted to play defense, so Brian stepped quickly toward the basket. Tyrone, who wasn't in the best physical condition of his life, nearly fell backward. Brian then leaped into the air and swished a jumper from about fifteen feet away.

"Way to shoot the ball, Davis," Lamont shouted.

Reggie's team then took over on offense. After several passes to Tyrone and Clarence, Reggie faked Tony out of his sneakers and drove to the basket for an easy lay-up. As the game progressed, Brian found the sweat on his body and the squeaking of the sneakers on the warped floor and the fast-paced basketball action made him feel as happy as he had felt in a long while. He was where he wanted to be, on a basketball court, and he loved every minute of it.

During the spirited half-court game, Brian tried to use his new offensive moves to the basket as often as he could. Once he received the ball in the right corner, faked up with the ball as if he were going to shoot one of his accurate jump shots, watched as Tyrone leaped slightly toward him—and then dribbled around Tyrone to the basket for a slam dunk.

"Man," said Clarence, his eyes wide behind his protective goggles, "nice move, homeboy."

Tyrone called time and high-fived Brian, while Reggie and the others congratulated him for making such a spectacular drive to the basket. Then Tyrone, huffing and puffing and perspiring freely, took the ball and showed Brian how to fake with his eyes and head to get his defender off balance.

"Many defensive players watch the ball or

your head or eyes," said Tyrone, cupping the ball in his two big hands. "Those dudes are the easiest to fake out of position. All you do is this." And as Brian pretended to be a defender who was being fooled, Tyrone demonstrated a few quick head bobs and eye movements, then drove to the basket for an easy lay-up.

"You gotta anticipate what the defensive man is going to do and then concentrate on making your best move to the basket," Tyrone called out.

LaMont, the team leader and a good driver to the basket himself, added, "You'll be able to fake most of the dudes we face right out of their jocks. But like Coach said, you gotta know what you're trying to do."

As the half-court game reached its final moments, Brian found himself faking better while still shooting as well as before. He drove hard to the basket against Clarence and Reggie as well as Tyrone. He knew this brief game wouldn't make him a better offensive player in one day. But he felt thrilled to be learning from one of the city's playground legends.

The half-court game ended with Brian's team winning by a couple of baskets, and with all the players soaked with perspiration and not looking forward to going out into the cold air again. As the screaming kids who had been watching ran onto the floor to play their own pickup games, Brian toweled off and accepted the congratulations of his teammates for his improved play.

"It'll take a while before you're really comfortable doing all the things we practiced tonight," Tyrone said. "But at least it's a start. And with that great outside shot of yours, it'll be only a matter of time." Tyrone's round face creased into a broad smile as he high-fived Brian.

"Yeah," added Reggie as he pulled on his winter coat, "but don't forget to pass the ball to the rest of us once in a while. You know, for old time's sake." He let out a high-pitched laugh, then high-fived Brian and Tyrone.

Brian thanked Tyrone and the toothless old caretaker for letting them use the community center. He started to walk out of the building with his teammates.

As they reached the doorway, Brian and the others looked up and saw two members of the professional NBA Indiana Pacers enter the building. One was seven-foot Artie Woodson, a muscular white center who had to duck to get through the doorway. The other was Wiley Patterson, a six-foot-five-inch sharpshooting guard. Brian had seen both of them on TV, but now he marveled at how big the two professional players really were as they stood next to him.

Tyrone, who knew both players, introduced them to Brian and his teammates, and then told them that both Woodson and Patterson spent many of their spare hours working with the community center's junior-league teams. Brian shook hands, and he could feel his mouth drop open as he stared at the two pro players.

Tyrone looked at Brian and smiled. "Maybe

next week you can try out your new moves against these guys," he said, nodding at the two professional players.

"Yeah, man," Reggie said, "show 'em a few things."

Reggie and Tony laughed, and Brian shook his head. He was a bit awestruck at having actually met a couple of professional players, and now Tyrone was talking about him going one-on-one against them.

But right now, he was thinking about the Patriots' next game when he could try out his new offensive moves.

THREE

At school on Monday, Brian and the other members of the Jefferson High varsity soon grew tired of answering the question "What went wrong against Gary Tech?" The Patriots' 85–70 loss in the first game of the big Terre Haute invitational tournament seemed to hurt the fans and students as much as it did the players and coaches. And hardly anybody mentioned the win over Clayville in the consolation game on Saturday night—or the thirty points Brian had scored.

"Man," Reggie said in the hallway as he and Brian and Tony were changing classes during the day, "we've won three out of four games this season, but the way everyone around here is talking you'd think we lost them all."

Only Mr. Bandiwell, Brian's homeroom

teacher and one of the chaperons who had traveled with the team to Terre Haute to supervise the varsity's stay at a Holiday Inn, was a little understanding. He seemed to realize how powerful the Gary Tech team really was and how difficult it would have been to defeat them at this stage of the season.

The tall, middle-aged homeroom teacher with black-rimmed glasses greeted Brian in the morning with a hearty handshake and said, "I'm really proud of you boys, Brian, even if that Gary Tech bunch was just too tough for us right now." Mr. Bandiwell pushed his glasses onto the bridge of his nose and added with a smile, "Maybe we'll meet those jumping jacks in the tournament and get some revenge."

And Lori Harper, the blond cheerleader who sat next to Brian in both homeroom and English class, applauded gently when Brian arrived at school. "Congrats on your thirty points in that Clayville game," she said. But then Brian saw her pretty face sag into a frown as she said, "What happened against Gary Tech?"

The rest of the day seemed to drag for Brian, and he had trouble concentrating on his schoolwork. Even Miss Pinchot, the narrow-faced English teacher, seemed to pick on him when he wasn't as prepared for class as he should have been. And after a while the comments of the students began bothering him, and he couldn't wait for the day to end and for basketball practice to begin. After all, he had some new offensive moves to work on now.

* * *

Brian, Reggie, and Tony were walking to the gym for practice, when Mr. Rhodes, the gray-haired principal, stopped them near the locker-room door. Brian noticed a broad smile on Mr. Rhodes's round face as he shook their hands vigorously.

"Now don't you boys worry," said the smiling principal, looking up at Brian. "Losing that game to Gary Tech was actually a wonderful thing." And he laughed to himself.

Brian, Reggie, and Tony exchanged puzzled glances.

"You see," continued Mr. Rhodes in his soft grandfatherly tone of voice, "twice before in the history of Jefferson High basketball, the boys' varsity team lost an early season game to a team from Gary. It happened during the 1968–69 season, and again in 1977–78. And at the end of both seasons, we went on to win the Indiana state basketball championship. Think about that, boys." Mr. Rhodes chuckled and walked away. The three teammates shook their heads on their way to the locker room. "Man," Reggie said, "that old dude's a walking basketball history book."

Brian began changing into his practice gear and looked around at the other players. All of them seemed to have survived the tough week-end loss at the Terre Haute tournament in good spirits and were ready to push on with the season.

Alvin Woolridge, sophomore black guard,

passed his basketball around his back again and again. "It's going to be real cool to play two home games this week. I've had my fill of bus trips for a while."

The sharpshooting guard, the team's best three-point bomber, began his Michael Jackson imitation and moonwalked backward to where redheaded senior guard Terry Hanson was studying a sheet of individual statistics Coach Ford had posted on a bulletin board.

"Hey, we're averaging seventy-three point three points a game," Alvin said, looking over Terry's shoulder. He studied the stats and continued in a playful voice by saying, "And look at me, man, averaging a big three point three points for our first four games."

"Yeah," Terry said, smiling, "but just think how many shots you put up. Your right arm must be tired from heaving all those three-point misses."

"Not me, man," Alvin said, flexing his shooting arm, "I can toss 'em up all day long." He playfully elbowed Terry in the ribs and laughed.

George Ross and Cisco Vega, graduates from last year's B team, joined the others looking at the stat sheet. Brian watched as Brad Cunningham, the team's resident brain and also a substitute, ambled over to the bulletin board and squinted through thick-lensed glasses at the figures on the single sheet of paper.

Clarence Reed, adjusting his protective goggles over his eyes, walked by on his way upstairs to practice and said with a smile, "Man, why is it that all the dudes without any numbers to speak of are always the ones most interested in the stat sheets?" He laughed and mounted the stairs leading to the main gym.

"Hey, Jackson," said Cisco, "you're leading the team in scoring with a cool twenty-two point three points a game." The smiling junior looked at Brian and added, "And Davis's averaging just over twenty points a game."

"Yeah, and Reggie's scoring ten point eight points a game," said Alvin.

LaMont continued walking and said in his usual even voice, "Only statistic that means anything to me is our won-lost record."

And with that last comment by their leader setting the tone for the day, Alvin and Terry and the rest of the varsity players left the stat sheet behind and headed for the gym. Brian, moody senior backup center Nick Vanos, and big senior Jeff Burgess—a football all-star as well as a member of the basketball team—brought up the rear.

After Brian and his teammates warmed up by shooting baskets and running twenty-five laps around the gym, their young head coach, Tom Ford, blew his whistle and called the players over to the midcourt circle. Coach Ford, a former star six-foot-three guard at Jefferson High who went on to become All-American at Purdue, looked down at his clipboard and opened the practice. Coach Williams stood beside him, as did the B-team coach, Pat Young, who usually gave the team a scouting report on their next opponent.

"Well, I suppose the weekend over at Terre

Haute could have been worse," Coach Ford said. "And by now I'm sure all of you are just as tired as Coach Williams and I are of trying to explain to people why we lost to Gary Tech."

LaMont and several other players shuffled their feet. Brian figured they were as embarrassed and as upset about the loss to Tech as he was. At least he hoped so.

"So let's forget about the Terre Haute tournament except to learn from whatever mistakes we might have made over there. And let's concentrate on the three games we have before Christmas vacation." Coach Ford checked his clipboard. "And as I'm sure you're aware, the next two games are here at our own gym."

"All right," Alvin said, nodding. "I like it."

"Yeah, man," Reggie added, "maybe now we can get some home cooking from the refs."

Coach Williams shook his head and said in his baritone voice, "We can't blame the officials for anything. Only bad teams cry about home cooking and stupid calls. Your only job is to practice hard and be the best you can be." The heavyset coach stroked his goatee and added, "Of course, you have an obligation to be good students, too."

Coach Ford nodded agreement. "That's right," he said in his usual calm manner. "But your attitude can drag the team down. Remember the Gary Tech game. Most of you were a little overconfident after we won our first two games of the season. We've got to approach every game from now on as if it were the finals of the state tournament and play as hard as we can."

Coach Ford then nodded at Pat Young, a history teacher and the B-team coach, who also was responsible for compiling most of the scouting reports on the varsity's upcoming opponents. Coach Young, a five-foot-seven third-year coach, opened the notebook he was carrying and looked up at Brian and the other varsity players.

"Tomorrow night," Coach Young began, pushing his glasses onto the bridge of his nose, "you'll be up against St. Francis, which, as most of you should know, is a small Catholic school over on the north side. And on Friday Southeast High'll be here." The little coach shuffled some papers inside his notebook. "But first, let's start with the St. Francis Braves."

And for the next ten minutes, Coach Young told Brian and the other players everything they should know about the team from St. Francis High School—including a player-by-player report, with each kid's strengths and weaknesses.

"St. Francis is a small, scrappy team," the coach said, "that likes to play zone defense most of the time. And their overall team quickness helps them play several zones during the course of each game. They don't have the height or enough top substitutes to play much man to man."

"And that's why we'll be working on our zone offenses and our outside shooting today after Coach Young's report," Coach Ford interjected. "But remember, too, that one of the best ways to defeat a zone defense is to fast-break it to death. Try to beat the other players down the floor before they have time to set up their zone." The coach looked at Brian, LaMont, and Clarence. "That means we need to control the boards," he added.

Clarence, one of the city's top-rated rebounders, nodded and smiled. "Man, those little dudes won't even *see* a rebound," he said, high-fiving with Alvin and Cisco Vega.

Coach Young turned the page of his notebook and continued with the scouting report. "As for the players to watch for at St. Francis," he said, pushing his glasses back onto the bridge of his nose again, "their top scorer so far this season is a kid named Adam Strump. He's a six-three forward, and he's also their top rebounder. He's a husky kid and takes up lots of space under the basket."

Coach Ford pointed at Clarence. "He's yours, big guy," the coach said. "We'll be playing our usual man-to-man defense, so shut this guy down and don't let him see a rebound."

"The dude's history," Clarence said.

"Their center," Pat Young continued, "is a skinny senior named Rich Stonebraker. He's about six five and doesn't do much on offense. But he's a real good defender under the basket in their zones, and he rebounds pretty well, too." The pasty-skinned B-team coach looked up and added, "But Davis shouldn't have any trouble with him if they play their usual zones."

Coach Young glanced back down at his notebook and continued. "Finally, the only other offensive threat for them is their six-foot-one guard, Allan Forrester." The coach looked up

and added, "He's one of the quickest playmakers we'll face this year."

Brian saw Coach Ford pointing at Reggie.
"He's all yours," the head coach said. "Shut him
off and their whole offense will bog down."

Reggie smiled. "The boy's in *serious* trouble,
man."

Coach Young finished by talking about the
small Catholic school's offensive system against
a man-to-man defense. Finally, the redheaded
B-team coach looked up from his notebook and
glanced at Coach Ford.

"All right," Coach Ford said, "if there are no
questions about the team we'll be facing tomorrow night, let's get to work."

And for the next hour and a half, Brian and
the other varsity players ran and shot and
dribbled and played tough man-to-man defense
in preparation for the following night's game.
Just before the end of practice, Coach Ford
motioned for Brian to join him near midcourt
for a chat, and he jogged over to join his coach.

"I heard your first session with Tyrone Russell was a success," Coach Ford said. "What did
you think?"

Brian wiped some perspiration from his forehead with the back of his hand. "Well, Tyrone
has more offensive moves than anybody I've
seen. He's already taught me a lot, and I'm really
looking forward to learning a whole lot more."

Coach Ford reached into the pocket of his
red-white-and-blue Jefferson High warm-up
jacket and extracted an envelope. "This is just
one of about two dozen letters I've received

from big-time college basketball programs asking me all about you. The others are in my desk drawer."

Brian just stared down at his coach, not really understanding. "I don't get it, coach," he said, scratching his head.

A big smile creased his coach's friendly face. "Brian, you're good enough right now that colleges are beginning to watch you in hopes you'll want to play basketball for them. You and Oscar Brown over at Westside, as well as big Dexter Cole up at Lincoln North, are the top three big men in the city, and all the college coaches'll soon be competing for you."

"But I'm only a junior."

"Sure, but that's when these college coaches start noticing the best players from all over the country, especially big kids like you." Coach Ford held up the envelope. "What I'd like to do is keep all these letters in my desk until after the season, and then you can look at them if you want to. I've done the same thing for all the college basketball prospects we've had here, and it's worked out well. It keeps you from becoming distracted and lets you concentrate on both basketball and your schoolwork."

Brian couldn't help feeling a tingle of excitement as he thought about two dozen college coaches actually being interested in him. "Sure, coach," he said, smiling, "whatever you say. You've got more experience in this kind of thing than I do."

"Just keep working on your skills," he said,

"especially with Tyrone. It will pay off for Jefferson and your future."

At the supper table later that evening, Brian couldn't help blurting out the news about the college recruiters to his mom and his Aunt Margaret, who both seemed pleased.

"But don't forget your schoolwork, either," his mom said, a slender pretty woman with short-cropped blond hair. Brian was glad she had grown accustomed to her new job as a medical secretary at the same downtown clinic where Aunt Margaret worked as a technician. And he was also glad that she seemed happy with their move from Paintville to the big city, even though he found she missed his dad as much as he did.

"Your mom's right," Aunt Margaret said from across the table. She looked like his mom but was taller and had graying hair. "None of those schools wants basketball players who are going to drop out of school because of bad grades." His aunt served Brian a second helping of mashed potatoes, then winked at him. "Of course, scoring thirty points a game won't hurt none either," she added with a chuckle.

Brian did his homework and went to bed early. He wanted to be well rested for the next night's game against St. Francis, and soon he was fast asleep and dreaming about game-winning baskets and thirty-point games—and college recruiters pounding on his front door.

FOUR

Even though the St. Francis game was on a weeknight, the three thousand–seat gymnasium was rapidly filling with excited fans from both schools. As Brian and his teammates walked toward the locker room, the girls' varsity teams from Jefferson and St. Francis were warming up on the court for the preliminary game.

Soon the girls' game was underway, and Brian and his teammates began changing into their white home uniforms for only the second time that season. The players sat in front of their lockers as they dressed and listened to Reggie and Tony talk about the St. Francis players.

"Man, Tony and I heard from a dude over at Northport High that these St. Francis guys are dirty players," said Reggie, pulling on his white jersey with the number fifteen.

Tony nodded. "Yeah, especially that Forrester guy, the six-one guard who Coach Young says is supposed to be so quick." Tony buttoned the jacket of his blue warm-up jacket, then added, "And I hear he likes to push and shove ya while you're trying to cut through their zone defenses."

Brian stood and straightened some wrinkles in the number fifty on his white jersey. "That's probably why their zone defenses are as tough as Coach Young said they were," he said. "Nobody gets through without being hit a few times."

Clarence adjusted his goggles on top of his head and flexed his elbows. "Those little guys better look out who they're messing with. That area under the hoop is *my* turf."

"Yeah, but hitting back at 'em is just what they want, bro," said LaMont, getting to his feet near his locker. "I've seen other teams do the same thing. It's the only way those little dudes can play with us. And if one of us gets kicked out of the game, then that's even better for them."

"LaMont's right," Coach Ford said as he and Coach Williams strode into the locker room. The players all sat for the usual pregame talk, and the coach continued. "Just play it cool and let the officials blow their whistles. If they don't, then I'll let them hear about it." He glanced at Clarence. "But whatever you do, don't hit back."

"And don't think these St. Francis kids can only win by playing dirty," Coach Williams said, stroking his goatee. "They're always one of the city's tough little schools, and every year they seem to cause a fair number of upsets."

For the next five minutes, Coach Ford quickly reviewed the St. Francis scouting report, then told the team that the starting lineup would be the same as it had been for the first four games of the season: Brian at center, LaMont and Clarence at the forwards, and Reggie and Terry at the guards. And he said he hoped the players off the bench began playing a little better than they had so far while the starters were resting.

As the girls' game upstairs in the gym reached the final few seconds, Coach Ford called the players together and they all put a hand into a huddle, then yelled "One, two, three, let's go!" and started to walk toward the stairs leading to the court.

"Man, I'm ready to play," Reggie said, looking up at Brian as they mounted the stairs. Brian could see the excitement in his friend's eyes. "I can just feel it."

"Me, too," Brian said, "but I got a funny feeling about this game. I mean, I don't think it's going to be so easy."

As soon as the victorious Jefferson girls' team and the losing St. Francis girls headed for their locker rooms, Brian and the others looked out through the glass door leading to the floor as the St. Francis boys' team took the court. They were dressed in classy green-and-white warm-ups with the face of an Indian brave decorating the back of each jacket. And while they began shooting lay-ups, their several hundred fans waved green-and-white pom-poms and cheered wildly. Brian saw several Catholic priests among the St. Francis rooters.

"There's Forrester," Tony said, "the one shooting the lay-up now."

Brian and the other players looked at the six-foot-one-inch St. Francis guard, who appeared lean and quick and a little cocky as he flipped a fancy shot up at the basket.

The Jefferson fans began chanting, "We want the Patriots! We want the Patriots! We want the Patriots!"

"Let's get these dudes," Reggie said.

Coach Ford opened the door leading to the gym and nodded at LaMont. "Let's go, guys!" he said. "Play hard."

As the Jefferson High pep band played the school's spirited fight song and the two thousand or so Patriots fans stood and cheered, Brian and his teammates jogged onto the floor to begin their warm-ups. As usual, the cheerleaders, including Lori Harper, ran alongside the players shaking red-white-and-blue pom-poms. And as always, all the hoopla caused nervous butterflies in Brian's stomach.

After fifteen minutes or so of lay-ups and jump shots, Brian dribbled the ball several times and spotted his aunt and mom sitting with Mr. Rhodes near the Jefferson players' bench. Brian smiled as his mother waved to him, then was shaken from his thoughts by Reggie, who tapped him on the arm.

"Man, I can't miss," Reggie said. "And my legs feel like springs. I'm gonna have me a great game."

Brian was beginning to sweat from swishing warm-up shot after warm-up shot. The buzzer sounded the two-minute warning, indicating the game was almost ready to start. Brian and his teammates trotted over to their bench. Soon the Jefferson High mascot, a student dressed in a colonial patriot's costume complete with a tricorn hat, walked onto the court followed by a three-student fife-and-drum corps holding an American flag.

As the large crowd rose to its feet for the playing of the National Anthem, Tony looked up at Brian. "There're some college recruiters here tonight," he said, nodding toward the bleachers across from them. "I heard the coaches talking to one of them before we came onto the court, and they mentioned your name."

Brian felt the butterflies flutter even more in his stomach. "Well, I reckon we'll just have to give 'em all a show to remember," he said, hoping his weak smile would hide his nervousness from his friend.

Following the pep band's Star Spangled Banner, Brian and his teammates watched as the starting five for the St. Francis Braves, dressed in their green-and-white road uniforms, were introduced by the PA announcer. Brian noticed the loud round of applause for the Braves' guard, Allan Forrester. Even louder applause echoed through the old gym as Brian and his fellow starting teammates were introduced to the fans.

"All right, guys," Coach Ford said as they huddled before heading out to start the game, "play hard and be prepared for their zone defenses. Take good shots, and move the ball around." The coach stuck out his hand, and Brian and the other players reached out and slapped theirs on top of the coach's. "Ready, one, two, three, let's go!"

"Go, Patriots, go! Go, Patriots, go!"

The Jefferson High cheer block screamed, and Brian's butterflies danced in his stomach as he walked out to the midcourt circle to jump against Rich Stonebraker, the St. Francis Braves' starting center. Brian looked at Stonebraker, a pencil-thin six-five senior, and offered his hand to him. The tall senior just scowled at Brian and looked at Allan Forrester and Adam Strump, his teammates on the other side of the jump circle, who were chuckling.

"Forget it, man," Reggie said, stepping up to Brian and whispering in his ear. "Let's get these dudes."

The game opened with Brian easily outjumping Stonebraker and tapping the ball to Reggie, who quickly began to dribble toward the Jefferson basket. As Reggie raced into the forecourt closely guarded by Jason Willoughby, the other St. Francis guard, Brian turned to run after them, but immediately felt Rich Stonebraker's elbow jab into his ribs, knocking the wind from his lungs.

Brian doubled over and tried to catch his breath. On the Jefferson bench, Coach Ford leaped to his feet and pointed at Brian, and then at Stonebraker, who was running after the other players. Since most of the fans in the gym were watching Reggie dribbling the ball, only a few of them spotted the flagrant foul against Brian. But fortunately for the Jefferson Patriots, one of the two officials saw Stonebraker's dirty play and whistled him for a foul.

Brian heard the short, balding official speak to Stonebraker. "I don't want to see any more of that stuff, son," he said. The official then turned to the scorer's table and said, "Flagrant foul on number forty-five in green, and a technical foul on number forty-five as well. We'll shoot two shots, plus the technical. Then it's white's ball out-of-bounds."

Reggie and LaMont stepped over to Brian to see if he was all right. Brian breathed deeply and nodded, then saw the St. Francis coach arguing with the official.

As Brian took his place at the free-throw line, Rich Stonebraker brushed past him, and Brian saw the smile on the skinny center's face. Clarence Reed, his eyes burning with anger behind his protective goggles, walked over and bumped up against Stonebraker.

"Man, you better watch your butt tonight," Clarence said in a deep voice resembling a growl, "or I'm personally going to kick it into the floor."

Allan Forrester and husky Adam Strump, the two other St. Francis stars, rushed over and began pulling the still-smiling Stonebraker away from Clarence. Both officials ran into the foul lane and tried to separate all the players, warning both Clarence and Stonebraker that they would be removed from the game if they continued the rough stuff.

"Man, this dude started it," said Clarence, pointing at Stonebraker and walking away from the foul lane.

Brian had never seen Clarence so angry, and he watched as LaMont stepped over to the big Jefferson forward and tried to calm him down.

As soon as order was restored, the referee told all of the other players to stand well behind Brian as he shot the three free throws. Jefferson was going to get the ball after the shots, so nobody was permitted on the foul lane.

Then Brian took a deep breath, accepted the ball from the official, and shot the first free throw—which struck the front of the rim and bounded away, much to the delight of the St. Francis players and fans.

"Way to go," Forrester said from behind Brian.

Reggie stepped over to Brian. "Just relax, bro," he said.

Brian nodded, made sure he bent his legs, and aimed at the basket. His second free throw, now that he was warmed up a little, swished through the basket. The Jefferson cheer block screamed with delight. Brian then aimed at the basket again, but his third shot struck the back rim, rolled around to the front, and then dropped off the hoop.

As the St. Francis players clapped and the officials brought the ball to the sidelines so Jefferson could inbound it, Brian shook his head. He figured he should have made all three free throws. He had never shot free throws so early in a game before, and he realized he hadn't been warmed up enough to be successful.

"Don't worry about it, man," LaMont said.

Brian nodded, and the game resumed with a toss-in from Clarence to Reggie, who passed the ball to the team's playmaker, redheaded Terry Hanson. As Brian ran under the basket and tried to get open, Terry dribbled the ball like a yo-yo. He seemed puzzled. Raising his hand for a pass, Brian saw that his other teammates were also trying to figure out what kind of defense St. Francis was using.

Brian soon realized that the St. Francis center was playing a tight man-to-man defense against him and was making it difficult for Terry to throw him a pass. The four other St. Francis defenders appeared to be playing some sort of zone against the remaining Jefferson players.

Finally, in his frustration, the usually calm and collected Terry risked a pass to Brian. Stonebraker reached out and deflected the ball to Allan Forrester, who turned and quickly began a fast break to the other basket. Terry swore to himself, and both teams raced downcourt.

It didn't take long for Brian to realize that Forrester was one of the quickest playmakers he had ever seen. The confident six-foot-one white guard zipped past Reggie as if the usually quick Jefferson guard was standing still, then laid the ball into the basket. Forrester turned to run back downcourt for defense and raised his fist in the air, then exchanged high-fives with

Stonebraker, Strump, and his other teammates.

Back at the other end of the court, Terry dribbled into the frontcourt and passed the ball to Reggie, who immediately tried to solve the St. Francis zone defense. For his part, Brian once again ran under the basket with his hands raised in an effort to free himself for a pass. But Stonebraker stuck to him like a shadow.

Cutting away from Stonebraker to a spot about fifteen feet from the basket, Brian finally freed himself from Stonebraker long enough for Reggie to fire a pass to him. But once he caught the quick chest pass, Brian found that both Stonebraker and Strump acted quickly and were on him so tightly he couldn't get off one of his accurate long jump shots.

Forcing a poor shot over the two defenders, Brian knew from the moment he released the ball that it wasn't going into the basket. In fact, the high-arching shot sailed over the hoop without touching anything and landed in Adam Strump's big hands. As the teams turned and raced toward the other basket, the St. Francis rooters yelled "Air ball!" at Brian.

At the other end of the court, Brian and his teammates allowed their frustration on offense to affect their defensive play. Terry was slow to get back to guard Jason Willoughby, and the St. Francis playmaker was free for a few moments to dribble down the foul lane without a defender.

Brian watched as Clarence stepped away from Strump, the man he was supposed to be guarding, and tried to stop Willoughby's drive down the middle. But the quick guard waited until Clarence leaped into the air for a blocked-shot attempt, then passed the ball to the now unguarded Strump, who sank an easy lay-up to give St. Francis a 4–1 lead.

The St. Francis fans cheered. Coach Ford called time.

Back on the bench, Brian and his teammates shook their heads and swore to themselves at their bad play so far. The coach just told them to calm down and get organized.

"On offense," Coach Ford said in his usual controlled voice, "you guys still haven't realized what kind of defense they're playing against us. It's a box-and-one, a four-man zone with Stonebraker playing man to man against Davis. It's the first time we've seen it this year, but I'm sure it's not going to be the last." The coach looked at Brian and added, "The word's out on you, and other teams are going to do everything they can to stop you from shooting the ball."

Brian toweled off, then said, "So what can we do?"

"Not too much right now," said Coach Ford. "We haven't worked against a box-and-one much this year in practice, so what we'll have to do tonight is use Brian more as a decoy than as an offensive weapon. The rest of you will have to pass the ball around until you see an opening in the four-man zone. And when Brian does manage to get a pass, he'll probably be double-teamed right away."

Coach Williams added, "And that means that one of you oughtta be wide open for an easy

shot. Just move the ball around and somebody
should get a good shot."

The game resumed, and the Jefferson players
followed Coach Ford's instructions perfectly.
While the four-man St. Francis zone defense
bothered Brian and LaMont, both of whom were
usually involved in all the Jefferson offensive
plays, Reggie and Terry and Clarence were open
most of the time and tried to take advantage of
it.

Terry shot and missed four times during the
remainder of the first quarter. One time, while
Jefferson had the ball, Reggie faked a pass to
Brian, causing the St. Francis zone to shift a
little, then swished a fifteen-foot jumper from
the top of the key. Another time, when he
noticed that the zone was too spread out,
Reggie drove down the middle of it and toward
the basket. He made a twisting lay-up, and was
fouled by Adam Strump in the process.

The first quarter ended in a tie: 14–14.

On defense, the Jefferson Patriots played a
tight man-to-man. While Forrester did manage
to break away from Reggie a few times for
lay-ups or short jumpers during the rest of the
half, the other St. Francis players found it
difficult to shoot over Brian and Clarence once
they got close to the basket.

For the remainder of the first half, the St.
Francis defense was successful in stopping
both Brian and LaMont—the top two Jefferson
scorers—from doing much damage. LaMont
managed only a single free throw during the
first two quarters, while Brian added a short

jump shot to the free throw he made to open the game.

And while Coach Ford kept the starting five in for most of the half—George Ross was the only sub, replacing Clarence briefly—only Reggie managed to solve the St. Francis defense. Scoring often on twisting drives to the basket and occasionally on long jump shots from the top of the key, Reggie led all scorers at half time with sixteen points.

The score at half time: Jefferson 29, St. Francis 27.

Brian, LaMont, and the other Jefferson players trudged with their heads down to the locker room knowing that they were being outplayed.

FIVE

"Man, we made those dudes look good," Reggie said in the locker room at half time. He slammed a towel onto the floor near his locker. "And the way they push and hit on defense is like getting mugged."

"Tell me about it," Brian said, slumping onto the bench in front of his locker. He held up his arms so Reggie could see them. "Look at all these red marks from Stonebraker's hands and elbows."

And although Brian didn't mention it, his pride was also bruised at having scored only three points in a half for the first time since grade school—and on a night when college scouts were watching.

Coach Ford followed the players into the locker room and raised his hands to quiet everybody down. "All right, listen up," he said. "That box-and-one defense they're using is pretty effective, so we'll have to come up with something to get some better scoring opportunities."

Coach Ford stepped over to the blackboard and began to draw several offensive plays. "We'll work more on this starting tomorrow at practice," the coach said, "but for now, try and set picks under the basket for Davis and Jackson to cut around." Brian watched as the young head coach drew several lines with his white chalk, before he stopped and looked at Brian and LaMont. "Both of you might be open for some shots along the baseline, but I doubt if you'll get a chance to drive at all. St. Francis is pretty quick." He turned and pointed at the blackboard again, drawing while he continued to talk. "Our best bet will probably be when they double-team either Brian or LaMont, leaving somebody else open for an easy shot."

Coach Ford looked at Alvin Woolridge, the sophomore guard with a good long-distance shooting touch. "Alvin," the coach said, "you're in for Terry to start the second half. If their zone gives you an outside shot, take it."

Brian thought he saw a gleam in Alvin's eyes.

"Come on, guys!" Cisco Vega said, clapping his hands. "Let's make it happen!"

As the team huddled up before taking the floor again, Coach Ford looked at Clarence and said, "Remember, try and keep your cool out there, too. Let them make the mistakes."

Brian looked up and saw the determination

on the faces of LaMont, Reggie, and Clarence just before they all yelled "One, two, three, let's go!" and headed back upstairs to the court.

The second half opened with St. Francis using the same box-and-one defense against Brian. But now Reggie and Alvin seemed to be open more often for easy jump shots as the defense clogged the area near the basket in an attempt to keep Brian and LaMont from scoring. As a result, the early part of the third quarter belonged to Jefferson.

Down the floor early in the period, Brian received a lob pass over Stonebraker's outstretched arms—and as soon as he was double-teamed by Adam Strump and Stonebraker, he snapped a pass to Alvin outside the three-point line. The sharpshooting guard then swished a long jumper, giving Jefferson a 35–31 lead.

The Patriots took their time to work Coach Ford's pick play. A quick pass to LaMont under the basket resulted in a double-team by the St. Francis defenders—allowing LaMont to zip a pass to Reggie back outside at the free-throw line for an easy fifteen-foot jumper. At one point, Reggie swished three jumpers in a row, making the score Jefferson 41, St. Francis 33.

Led by Forrester and Strump, the St. Francis Braves stormed back. A quick driving lay-up past Reggie by Forrester, a tap-in by Strump on a missed shot by Stonebraker, and another quick move and a jump shot by Forrester during the last minute of the quarter led to a 45–45 tie at the end of three periods.

The final quarter opened with both teams using the same lineups that had opened the second half. Forrester tried to drive on Reggie, but Alvin slapped the ball away. Brian tried a quick pass to Reggie at the free-throw line, but Stonebraker stole the ball. Strump pump-faked with the ball several times, but Clarence refused to be fooled and blocked the shot back into the big forward's face.

Midway through the final quarter, Reggie and Alvin began a shooting exhibition. First, Reggie hit a long three-point shot from past the top of the key. Then Alvin, after receiving a sharp pass from Brian, swished a three-pointer from near the left sideline. And finally, after Forrester had raced back on defense to foil one of Jefferson's few fast breaks of the game, Alvin passed the ball to Brian, who passed to LaMont—who zipped a hook pass to Reggie at the top of the key. Reggie swished a jump shot and turned to run downcourt with his fist raised in victory. Jefferson's cheer block yelled, as the score rose to Jefferson 54 and St. Francis 48 with just over two minutes to play.

St. Francis called time-out, their first of the game.

"We got 'em now!" cried Reggie, high-fiving with Cisco Vega, Nick Vanos, and the other subs.

Brian slumped onto the bench beside Reggie and tried to listen to Coach Ford over the loud music of the Jefferson pep band. He suddenly realized he had played the entire game so far and had passed the ball pretty well, even if he hadn't scored at all in the final half. But as he drank some Gatorade from a plastic squeeze bottle, he also thought about the college recruiters on hand and wondered with a smile if any of them had expected to see him as a playmaker.

"Okay, guys, play tough defense and on offense watch out for a fullcourt press," Coach Ford said finally. "It's getting late, and I figure they'll try and go after the ball whenever they have a chance. So be patient and make good passes."

Brian dragged his tired body back onto the court, and noticed that all five of the St. Francis starters, their uniforms soaked to a dark green with perspiration, were also walking a bit more slowly than usual.

St. Francis's Strump inbounded the ball to Forrester near midcourt, and the quick guard dribbled to the right of their basket with Reggie hounding him every step of the way. Before Brian realized what was happening, St. Francis worked a set play they had obviously planned in their huddle.

Brian was guarding Stonebraker when out of the corner of his eye he spotted Strump running toward him. At the same moment, Stonebraker cut for the basket. Before Brian could react, he slammed into the pick set by Strump on his left. The pick freed Stonebraker for an easy lay-up when nobody switched on defense to pick up Brian's man.

The score was Jefferson 54 and St. Francis 50, with a minute and a half remaining in the game.

"Press! Press!" St. Francis's coach yelled.

Before Brian and his teammates could set up their offense, Forrester stole Clarence's quick pass to Reggie. The St. Francis guard turned and drove to the basket, shot a spinning lay-up, and was fouled by Clarence, who had just stepped inbounds after making the errant pass to Reggie.

The St. Francis fans stood and applauded, while Coach Ford called time-out.

"Listen," the coach said calmly once Brian and the others were gathered around him, "don't lose your cool out there. You know their press is coming, so if Forrester makes his free throw, set up this play. Reed will inbound the ball to Davis near the free-throw line, and at the same time Dupree will use a pick by Woolridge and take off downcourt for a pass from Davis." The coach looked at Reggie. "Take your time and make the lay-up at the other end."

"No sweat."

The buzzer sounded to end the time-out, and the players from both teams trudged onto the court again. Forrester took his time at the free-throw line, then calmly swished his foul shot. The score was now Jefferson 54, St. Francis 53, and only sixty-seven seconds remained in the game.

"Press!" the tall St. Francis coach screamed.

"Do it! Do the play!" Coach Ford shouted.

Clarence grabbed the ball, faked a pass to Reggie, and then inbounded the ball with a looping pass to the jumping Brian that none of the shorter St. Francis players could reach.

Brian knew he was going to be double-teamed, so before he returned to the floor, he turned and spotted Reggie racing downcourt all alone with his left hand raised for a pass.

Brian tossed a pass with a bit too much arc on it, and by the time Reggie received the ball and was driving to the basket, Stonebraker had caught up with him. The St. Francis center pushed Reggie with both hands, stopping the lay-up and sending Reggie sprawling hard onto the floor under the hoop.

The Jefferson fans screamed, and the officials blew their whistles. "Son, that's a technical foul," the official shouted. "And you're out of the game."

Brian rushed over to where Reggie was trying to get to his feet. "You all right?" Brian asked, helping his friend limp over to the free throw line. Reggie nodded and flexed his shooting hand, grimacing a little with pain.

At the same time, the other official and Coach Williams were trying to keep Clarence from tearing Stonebraker apart. "I warned you, man!" Clarence shouted. "You didn't have to do that!"

After a St. Francis time-out, order was finally restored, and Reggie calmly sank three free throws in a row—two for the foul and one for the technical on Stonebraker—making the score Jefferson 57, St. Francis 53.

"All right!" Alvin shouted, high-fiving Reggie. "We got this game now!"

Then with only forty-nine seconds remaining to play, Clarence inbounded the ball to Reggie following the technical foul. St. Francis's fight seemed to have left them following Stonebraker's ejection from the game. Nevertheless, St. Francis tried hard to steal the ball from Brian and his teammates, but couldn't intercept Jefferson's sharp passes around the court. The seconds kept ticking away. With ten seconds remaining, Brian spotted Alvin standing wide open in the far corner of the forecourt. He tossed a looping crosscourt pass, which Alvin grabbed and tossed into the basket from about ten feet away.

The Jefferson fans rose and cheered, and except for a last-second lay-up at the buzzer by Forrester, the scoring was finished. The final score was Jefferson 59, St. Francis 55.

Exhausted but happy, Brian accepted congratulations from his teammates in the locker room, even though he had scored only three points—and none at all in the second half. Looking at the scorebook, Brian noticed that, just as Reggie had predicted, the guard led all scorers with his best game of the season so far: thirty-three points. He was followed by sharp-shooting sophomore, Alvin Woolridge, with sixteen. But like Brian, LaMont—the team's leading scorer with a twenty-two-points-per-game average—was held to only three points by the tough St. Francis defense. And for St. Francis, Adam Strump scored eighteen points and Allan Forrester seventeen.

"Well," Coach Ford said, "it wasn't a thing of beauty, but we'll take it. After all, a win is a win."

And despite his own poor scoring game and his inability to use his new offensive moves against the zone, Brian thought as he peeled off his sweaty white uniform, at least the team's won-lost record improved to four wins and only one loss. And that was some consolation after a long and frustrating game.

The following day was unseasonably warm for early December. Brian, Reggie, and Tony actually wore light jackets to school and ate their lunches in the sunshine on the school's concrete football bleachers. And all during the school day, the students were so giddy and pleased with the basketball team's successful record so far that to Brian it seemed like the school was infected with spring fever in December.

At practice after school, Coach Ford let the players shoot around for a while, then called them to the center-jump circle. "St. Francis's box-and-one defense sort of caught us off guard last night," the coach said. "I accept the blame for that, and all I can say is that it won't happen again."

Coach Williams said, "I saw several scouts from various high schools here in the city taking notes. Southeast had a guy sitting in the stands, and you can be sure he saw what St. Francis's box-and-one did to Brian and LaMont."

"So be ready to see the same kind of defense on Friday night," Coach Ford added. "But this time we'll be ready for them. Today, and especially tomorrow, you'll be learning an offense that'll destroy any box-and-one they use." The coach paused. "These other schools all know how tough it is for us to win without LaMont and Brian as important parts of our offense."

"Dupree and Woolridge sure saved our butts last night," LaMont said. "Way to shoot the ball. You guys scored forty-nine of our fifty-nine points."

"Man, that deserves some applause," Brian added.

As Reggie and Alvin smiled sheepishly, Brian and the others gave the two of them an ovation.

"But don't let it go to your heads," said Coach Ford.

The players all laughed, and Tony said, "Yeah, I bet nobody else will get a shot for the rest of the season."

The remainder of the brief practice was fairly easy, except for the entire squad running laps every time a player missed a free throw at the end of the session.

As the players headed for the locker room, Coach Williams caught up with Brian and said, "Tyrone called me last night after the game. He's free this evening and wants to know if you guys can get together again after supper here at the school."

Brian looked at the heavyset assistant coach and smiled. "I guess, but after last night's game he oughtta give me lessons in how to be a playmaker for all the moves I made. It was like watching everybody else play offense."

Coach Williams smiled. "Don't worry about it. Just consider last night's game a learning expe-

rience. You'll have other chances to show everybody the moves Tyrone has taught you."

"You're getting it, man," Tyrone said, perspiration dripping off his broad black face. "Just a
few more of these sessions and you'll be ready
to kick some butts on your own. Man, with your
outside shooting nobody'll be able to stop you
from scoring."

Brian and Tyrone had been shooting baskets
for about half an hour before they practiced
offensive moves to the basket. Tyrone showed
Brian the leg-hooking maneuver, the jab-step,
and several other tricks to help him gain an
advantage over the defensive man guarding
him. They also reviewed the art of faking and
feinting with the eyes, head, and ball. And then,
for an hour or so, Brian had worked on the
moves against Tyrone.

In the middle of Brian's final play, a second
ball zipped onto the court from the dark sidelines.

"Heads up!"

Brian and Tyrone looked up as they bumbled
both balls to see Reggie and Tony laughing.

"Where'd you guys come from?" Brian said,
grabbing one of the bouncing balls and hurling
it crosscourt at Reggie.

"Your mom said you'd be here with Tyrone, so
we thought we'd show you how it's done."

"No way, Dupree," Tyrone said, walking over
to his sweats on the bleacher. "My man Davis
here'll run your butt ragged."

Brian smiled. "How about we show these guys, Tyrone?"

"You show 'em, hotshot," Tyrone said, pulling on his sweats. "I got a long bus ride home."

"Okay, homeboy," Reggie said. "You're on."

Reggie and Tony took off their jackets and headed out to the court. Brian walked over to the former Jefferson star.

"Hey, thanks for the time."

"No sweat, my man," Tyrone said, straightening his wool cap. "Just keep 'em guessing." He headed for the door.

"Davis, we're getting too hot to handle out here," Tony shouted over at Brian. "You playing or what!"

They shot baskets and played halfcourt for a while and discussed the recently released high school basketball ratings in that day's newspaper.

"Man, Gary Tech is ranked number two in the state," Reggie said, looking over Tony's shoulder as he passed to Brian. "Marianville is still the top-rated team. No way those country boys can handle Tech's full-court press."

"Only two teams from Indianapolis are ranked in the top twenty," Brian said. "Westside is number eight and Lincoln North is number seventeen."

"Man, we belong in the top twenty," Tony said.

Brian swished a long jump shot, then turned and said, "Yeah, right. Who's going to put us in the rankings after we beat a team like St. Francis by only four points?"

But," Reggie said, shaking his head, "we're better than those dudes at Lincoln North."

Brian hit another jumper. "I reckon we'll get our chance to prove it next Tuesday up at Lincoln. But for now, we better take care of Southeast on Friday."

Tony joined Brian and swished a short jumper. "Those guys are nothing but a bunch of wimps," the bushy-haired junior said. "They haven't won a game yet this season."

Brian finished his workout and toweled off. "Yeah, but don't forget Terre Haute. We figured we were going to have it easy and those boys took us apart." He looked at his teammates. "The only way we can make the top twenty is to earn it."

SIX

In homeroom the next morning, blond cheer-leader Lori Harper, a girl from a small town who had moved to the big city a year before Brian, smiled as she took her seat next to him. Lori had helped Brian adjust to Jefferson High during the first few months of school. ˮ

"Guess what?" she asked.

Brian shrugged. He always felt awkward around girls. "I don't know, but I bet you're going to tell me."

"I've been selected as a tutor for the kids playing winter sports who are having trouble with their grades. It'll be lots of work, but my parents think it's something of an honor to be chosen. What do you think, Brian?"

He smiled. "Do you specialize in basketball players?"

She looked at him strangely for a moment, then laughed and punched him playfully on the arm. "You know it wouldn't be fair for me to favor one sport over another, although I will be helping Clarence Reed and Terry Hanson with their English. They're both doing pretty bad."

"Are they . . . flunking?" Brian asked, suddenly imagining both players becoming ineligible for basketball.

He watched as Lori looked around, then whispered in his ear. "I'm not really supposed to say anything, but they're both barely passing." She looked at him. "How are your grades?"

Brian shrugged. "Okay, I guess. Even in Miss Pinchot's English class." He chuckled. "I've never read so many books in my life. But I'm handling it okay."

The rest of the day passed slowly as Brian tried hard to concentrate on his schoolwork. But he couldn't get his poor scoring in the St. Francis game off his mind. He was looking forward to practice that afternoon—and to the game against Southeast on Friday night.

At practice, Coaches Ford and Williams were on a mission to make sure the team could defeat the box-and-one defense. They spent nearly an hour explaining and demonstrating a new offense designed to overcome the defense meant to stop Brian from becoming a scoring threat.

"This offense is nothing more than a series of picks and screens, mostly along the baseline, so that Davis and Jackson can get open for their shots," Coach Ford said. "And if they're open for a moment and then are suddenly double-teamed, then the rest of you should be in the clear to receive a pass.

"But if we run this offense correctly, that is, if we make good picks, then Davis should be free to take those jumpers of his. And both Jackson and Davis should be able to drive against the four-man box zone.

"So let's work five against five for half an hour or so," Coach Ford concluded, checking his watch, "and then Coach Young'll have some things to say about Southeast's team."

"And remember," Coach Williams added, stroking his black-and-silver goatee, "Southeast saw how well St. Francis's box-and-one messed us up on Tuesday night, so let's work hard today and see if we can't rig up a little surprise for those dudes."

"Yeah, let's make it lethal," Reggie said, high-fiving with Coach Williams.

And for the remainder of practice, Brian and his teammates worked on the new offense. Cisco, Brad, and the other substitutes played a box-and-one defense while the starters tried to overcome it with the new offense—and did, as Brian and LaMont used the many picks and screens set by Terry and Reggie and Clarence to get free for jumpers and drives to the hoop.

During a break in the action, Brian noticed that Nick Vanos, the dark-haired senior backup center, was absent, and he asked Tony about it. "Nick's got trouble at home again," Tony said, sipping water at one of the coolers in the gym. "You know, with his dad. His old man spent three weeks in an alcoholic rehab center, but now that he's back home Nick's probably catching hell."

Brian nodded sadly, since both Nick Vanos and he had something in common—an alcoholic father—although Brian's dad had never been violent. Nick, on the other hand, often came to school with cuts and bruises on his face. Although Brian and Nick had had a misunderstanding during the basketball tryouts, when Nick lost the center spot to Brian, they'd become friends since. Brian hoped Nick would be back at practice soon, and without his bruises.

Brian soon found that the new offense allowed him to use some of the shake-and-bake offensive moves Tyrone Russell had taught him. Several times during the practice session, Brian cut past picks by Reggie, Terry, or Clarence and received a quick pass—then faked, feinted, and jab-stepped his way to the basket for a driving lay-up or a slam dunk. He faked a drive to the basket, getting George Ross, who was designated as the player chasing Brian man to man, off balance for just a moment. Then he leaped into the air and swished one of his accurate jump shots.

"Dy-no-mite," Reggie said, high-fiving Brian.

"Great moves," Coach Ford said, smiling. "Tyrone's got you flying high."

"Hey, man, save some of those moves for me," LaMont called out.

B-team coach Pat Young joined them after the players had cooled down a bit, and he began the scouting report on the Southeast Cougars by smiling at Brian and the others.

"Fellas," the short, pasty-skinned coach said as he pushed his glasses onto the bridge of his nose, "I usually don't say this, but these guys from Southeast are horrible. They've lost all five of their games so far this year, and if you don't beat them by twenty points, I'll be disappointed." The redheaded coach opened his notebook, then looked up again. "But then again, if you don't take every team seriously, you could lose even to a team like this."

And for the next ten minutes, Coach Young told them all about the Southeast Cougars. "Their tallest player is Gary Simmons, a six-four white forward, who's also their leading scorer. A six-three black kid named Nelson Moore plays center."

Brian heard Reggie burst into one of his high-pitched cackles. "Man, that Nelson Moore is pitiful," he said, shaking his head. "The dude can't do anything but jump, and on offense he can't dribble or shoot to save his life. I've been playing against him since we were kids."

Coach Ford cleared his throat. "I've heard these Southeast kids are young and inexperienced. But you guys know that if we're going to be the type of team we're all hoping to be, then we can't let down against anybody."

"And," Coach Williams added, "if you guys on the bench who haven't been playing much lately get into the game, then it'll be a good chance for you to play a little better than you have so far

...his season. When our starters come out for a rest, we fall apart."

Brian watched as Coach Ford nodded. "In any event, I expect everybody to show up tomorrow night with the proper mental attitude. With this new offense we practiced today, I figure there's no team in the city that can stop us now. It's all up to us."

"All right!" Cisco Vega said, clapping his hands.

"Let's do it to Southeast!" Terry Hanson shouted.

Then Coach Ford had Brian and the others warm up by shooting some lay-ups for five minutes before they ran some three-man and four-man fast breaks down the full length of the court. This was one of the team's favorite drills. Brian and his teammates loved to run and pass and get out on the break.

As Brian ran in a threesome that included Reggie in the middle and Jeff Burgess on the other wing, he noticed that Jeff was limping slightly. When they reached the hoop, Reggie tracked down the basketball and began the return fast break toward the other basket. But Brian saw that Jeff was really hurting and called out to Reggie to let the next group of three run their fast break.

Brian stepped over to where Jeff was flexing his right knee. "You all right?" he asked, noticing the pained expression on Jeff's face.

The big football player nodded, and said in his usual soft voice, "It's a football injury. Acts up once in a while. But I'll be all right after the pain goes away."

But as the two of them jogged back to the three lines on the other end of the court, Jeff's knee buckled, and the big guy grimaced with pain. Coach Williams ran over, and he helped Jeff to the locker room for some ice and a knee wrap.

"I guess that's just what we need," Brian said to Reggie as they returned to the fast-break lines. "With Vanos having trouble at home and with Jeff's knee acting up, that leaves us without a backup center."

"That's cool, man," Reggie said. "I'm available to step into the pivot." He playfully demonstrated his hook shot. But even Reggie's good-natured kidding couldn't hide the fact that Brian might have to get used to playing the entire game without a break.

SEVEN

At Jefferson High School throughout the next day, Brian could feel the excitement mounting for the second home basketball game of the week. The students were acting even crazier than usual for a Friday afternoon, plastering the school with Beat Southeast posters, and even the teachers seemed to be in the mood for the game.

Miss Pinchot also had the spirit. When Brian entered her room for English class, he saw the usually reserved teacher wearing a white tricorn hat and shaking a red-white-and-blue pom-pom.

During last period, he glanced out the window and noticed some snow flurries blowing in the cold afternoon breeze. The combination of wintry basketball weather and the cheerleaders practicing their yells in the hallways got his adrenaline flowing, and suddenly he could barely wait for the game.

Brian ate his usual pregame meal with his mom and his aunt that night, then walked through the blowing light snow with Reggie and Tony to the Jefferson gym. Both of his friends seemed less talkative and more determined than usual, and Brian was sure the Patriots were going to play a good game.

As the boys approached the school, he saw long lines of supporters from Southeast High buying tickets, their blue-and-white pom-poms giving away their identities. A dozen or so were already practicing loud cheers for their team.

"They must have hundreds of fans," Tony said.

"Yeah, man," said Reggie, pulling his knit cap farther down on his head, "and by listening to 'em you'd never know their team was oh and five for the season."

Brian followed his two friends through the players' entrance and said, "They'll be oh and six after tonight."

Reggie laughed, and both he and Tony high-fived Brian.

As the B teams of the two high schools played the preliminary game, the Patriots met in the locker room and changed into their home whites. Several minutes later, Coaches Ford and Williams arrived and began to review the scouting report.

"Southeast should open with a box-and-one zone defense," Coach Ford said, checking the notes in his clipboard, as he paced back and forth. "And, of course, if that's the case, then you all know what to do."

Brian heard somebody running into the locker room, and all of the players turned and saw Nick Vanos, his face bruised and his lips puffy, as he slowed to a stop and looked at the coaches. As Brian watched, Nick looked down at the floor as if to hide his face and his embarrassment.

"Coach, I'm . . . I'm sorry I'm late," Nick stammered.

The locker room was as quiet as a cemetery. Coach Ford paused for a moment, then said in an understanding voice, "You'd better get your uniform on, Nick."

Coach Ford cleared his throat. "Listen, guys," he said, "we all know Southeast is probably the city's weakest team this year. But remember: if you go into a game thinking you're going to beat up on a team, they could surprise you and kick your butts. So play hard all game long," Coach Williams concluded.

And as Brian and the other players stretched their muscles in the locker room and awaited the conclusion of the B-team game, Brian stepped over to where Nick Vanos was still changing into his uniform. The big, dark-haired senior looked up at him, and Brian saw the ugly red welts on his face.

"Are you okay?" Brian asked. He was genuinely concerned about the six-foot-four-inch center.

Nick just nodded numbly and continued dressing.

The B-team game ended a minute or so later. Brian and his teammates cheered when they learned Coach Young's inexperienced squad had defeated Southeast by a point. And as the two B teams were leaving the gym above them, Coach Ford gathered the varsity together in the locker room for a victory shout before they mounted the stairs to the nearly packed gymnasium.

Brian and his teammates trotted onto the court amid a roar from the more than two thousand Jefferson rooters. The Jefferson pep band filled the gym with a rousing number, and the cheerleaders leaped all over the floor. All the enthusiasm caused Brian to be so keyed up he almost missed seeing his mom and his aunt sitting near the bench.

As the buzzer sounded to indicate two minutes to game time, Brian and his teammates trotted to the bench and listened to Coach Ford's final comments. Brian removed his blue warm-ups and saw from the faces of LaMont and Clarence that they were as determined as he had ever seen them. Following the introduction of the starting lineups and the playing of the National Anthem, Brian and the same five starters took the floor.

Brian walked over to the center-jump circle for the opening tap and glanced at the short and seemingly inexperienced Southeast Cougars.

The baby-faced visitors were dressed in their blue away uniforms. Reggie stepped over to Brian and whispered in his ear.

"Man, these dudes are nothing," Reggie said.

Terry Hanson walked over and added, "Let's take it to 'em and blow the game open right away."

As the players from Southeast lined up for the opening jump ball, Brian checked numbers and identified their six-foot-three center, Nelson Moore, as well as their six-four scoring leader, Gary Simmons. The remaining players seemed awfully young and sort of lost out on the court, so Brian didn't pay much attention to them.

As the Jefferson band played and the cheerleaders from both schools clapped and screamed and stomped their feet, one of the two officials prepared to toss the ball up between Brian and Nelson Moore, the Southeast center. Brian suddenly noticed that LaMont was nodding to him, trying to get his attention. Almost immediately, Brian saw that the young Southeast player near Reggie had lined up on the wrong side of him, and also that LaMont was free to receive the tap. Brian and LaMont then both looked at Reggie, who nodded in recognition of the situation.

"Go, Patriots, go! Go, Patriots, go!"

The fans were going wild. Brian was ready to jump.

The official checked with the scorer and the timer, then tossed the ball in the air between Brian and Nelson Moore. Brian leaped as high as he could, stretching his six-foot-eight-inch frame to its fullest, and just managed to out-jump Moore. He tapped the ball to the wide-open LaMont, who pivoted quickly and spotted Reggie cutting downcourt toward the Jefferson basket.

LaMont passed the ball to Reggie, who slam-dunked it.

Brian's ears hurt as the Jefferson fans roared and the pep band's drummer pounded away on his kettledrums.

Brian began to run downcourt on defense, but turned and looked over his shoulder as the stunned Southeast Cougars tried to inbound the ball directly under the basket. Reggie, hanging downcourt in a one-player full-court press, sud-denly stole the inbounds pass and laid the ball into the basket. The game was only ten seconds old, and already the score was Jefferson 4, Southeast 0.

Again the fans roared and the drummer pounded.

Reggie ran upcourt to join his teammates and received high-fives from all of them. Brian smiled and said, "Way to go," before he, too, high-fived Reggie and turned to play defense on the approaching Southeast Cougars.

The first five minutes of the game belonged to Jefferson. The Southeast players immediately had problems against the Patriots' clinging man-to-man defense, and when they tried to drive down the middle to the basket, Brian, LaMont, and Clarence either intimidated them or blocked their shots. Until later in the quarter, the usual routine at the Southeast end of the

court would be a shot or a drive by their top
scorer Gary Simmons or their short playmaker
Andy Heller, which would be batted away by the
Jefferson Patriots if it didn't go wild.

On offense, Jefferson quickly demolished
Southeast's box-and-one defense with the new
plays they had learned in practice. The four-
man zone with six-three Nelson Moore playing
man-to-man on Brian was slow moving. Moore
had little success in staying with Brian—who
dazzled the crowd with his newly learned offensive moves.

After Reggie opened the game with his two
baskets, the Jefferson offense either ran fast
breaks for lay-ups by Terry, LaMont, or Reggie
or passed the ball to Brian, who couldn't miss.
Terry passed the ball to Reggie who flipped an
over-the-head pass to LaMont, who floated a
high pass over the short players in the zone to
Brian in the corner. Brian saw the out-of-control
Nelson Moore leaping at him on defense, so he
used several of Tyrone Russell's head-and-
shoulder fakes and watched as Moore jumped
in the air expecting a shot. Brian then dribbled
twice around the Southeast defender, took two
giant steps to the basket, and slammed the ball
through the hoop. Four other times, Brian received the ball easily and either swished long
jump shots or used shake-and-bake moves to
drive to the hoop for wide open lay-ups.

The score after five minutes: Jefferson 18,
Southeast 2.

Southeast's coach finally called time-out, and

Brian and his teammates ran over to their bench. They were greeted by high-fives from all the substitutes, as well as from the coaches. Brian had scored ten points on dazzling drives to the hoop and on accurate jumpers from long distance.

"Man, we can pound these guys into the floor," Reggie said, wildly high-fiving everybody.

"Way to go, guys," Coach Ford said. "Now you're looking like a team out there."

The quarter continued with the same lineups for both teams, and what followed was more of the same. Southeast finally managed to score four additional baskets on long jumpers. But Brian answered by swishing a three-point jump shot from about twenty-five feet, and Clarence hauled in his tenth rebound and then dunked the ball through the hoop so hard that the basket support shook for nearly a minute.

After one period: Jefferson 23, Southeast 10.

The game was such a rout so early on, that Coach Ford barely spoke to the players between quarters. He substituted Nick for Brian, Alvin for Reggie, and George for Clarence to start the second period. But the result was the same, as the Southeast subs couldn't even handle Jefferson's bench players.

Southeast abandoned their box-and-one defense and tried to play man to man, without much success. And although the Patriots' substitutes performed as poorly as they had all season long (only Alvin scored a basket), LaMont continued his fine play, scoring twelve points in the second quarter on spinning drives, fast-break lay-ups, and short jump shots.

Only forward Gary Simmons played well for the stumbling Southeast Cougars, scoring twelve points on jump shots over George Ross and an occasional rebound over Nick Vanos, followed by a tap-in. Nelson Moore, their unco-ordinated center, hit only one of ten shots in the first half and could manage only two rebounds against Clarence and the other Jefferson front-line players.

With three minutes remaining in the first half and the Jefferson Patriots leading 31–17, Coach Ford motioned for Brian to return to the game along with Tony and Cisco Vega at the guards. The coach also motioned Jeff Burgess into the game as a forward, since the big senior wanted to play despite his gimpy right knee. As Brian and the others were waiting at the scorer's table for a chance to enter the game, Coach Ford walked over and knelt beside Brian.

"They're playing man-to-man now," the coach shouted over the cheers and the band music, "so it might be a good chance for you to try some more of those shake-and-bake moves."

Brian nodded. The buzzer sounded.

As the Patriots inbounded the basketball and headed downcourt to start their offense, Tony began dribbling to his left just over the midcourt line, then quickly used a crossover dribble and raced toward the foul lane on his right. The Southeast players converged on the dribbling Jefferson guard, and at the last moment he passed the ball to Brian in the right corner.

Alone, about seventeen feet from the hoop, Brian aimed, leaped into the air, and launched a high-arching jump shot that swished through the basket, barely touching the net.

Score: Jefferson 33, Southeast 17.

As Brian ran downcourt to play defense, he heard the Jefferson cheer block yelling his name before the band's drummer drowned them out. And the recognition from his fans made him smile and feel happy inside.

As Southeast began their offense against the Patriots' tight man-to-man defense, Cisco, going for the steal, missed the ball and allowed the Cougars's Gary Simmons to swish a ten-foot jumper from the left side of the lane.

Jeff Burgess, wearing a knee brace, limped after the loose ball and passed it to Tony, who dribbled quickly upcourt. After raising his hand on the right side of the court, Brian received a pass from Tony over the outstretched arms of the young six-foot-two substitute center guarding him.

Brian turned and faced the blond kid, who immediately began watching Brian's head and shoulders. Recalling Tyrone's various lessons about fakes and feints, Brian shook his head and rolled his eyes, and the young defender rose slightly off his feet. Before the other Cougar defenders could arrive and offer defensive help, Brian took a giant step toward the baseline and was around the young blond kid. He dribbled twice, leaped into the air, and after gliding under the basket, raised the ball above and behind his head, and slammed in a reverse dunk from the other side of the hoop.

The Jefferson fans went wild, and Coach Ford smiled.

Reggie ran up to Brian. "Man, what a jam!"

The first half ended with the score Jefferson 41 and Southeast 19. Brian led all scorers with twenty points, his best total for a half so far. LaMont had added eleven.

As Brian trotted to the locker room with his teammates, he saw the young Southeast players trudging off the floor with their heads down, defeated. In contrast, the Patriots' locker room was once again filled with smiles and laughter —and confidence.

"Where are those college recruiters tonight?" Brian asked Tony, high-fiving with him and enjoying the team's big half-time lead. "We're burying these little guys!"

Nothing really changed in the second half, except that Coach Ford used his substitutes more, especially in the last quarter. Early in the third quarter, however, Brian and LaMont ran wild again, scoring easily on jump shots and spectacular drives to the basket. Near the end of the quarter, Coach Ford sent Nick into the game at center, with George Ross and Brad Cunning-ham, the team's "brain," at forward. Tony and Alvin played guard.

But once again, the Jefferson subs played poorly, and Southeast outscored the Patriots by five for the period, making the score 52–35 after three quarters. The lead was safe, Brian knew, but Coach Ford was obviously upset.

"Look, guys," the coach barked at the end of the third quarter, "we'll soon be playing some tough teams, and we'll need some subs to give the starters a rest once in a while." Brian thought he saw a worried look on Coach Ford's face. "This is our sixth game, and you guys sitting on the bench should be contributing more to our effort."

Despite the big lead, Brian and the other starters returned to open the final quarter. They used the opportunity to run some more plays. Reggie faked and feinted several times and left his young Southeast defender behind as he drove to the basket for an easy lay-up. Clarence blocked a shot by Nelson Moore at one end of the court, then raced down the floor and arrived at the Jefferson basket in time to tap in a missed jump shot by Terry Hanson. Brian worked a perfect pick-and-roll play with Reggie, cutting to the basket after picking off Reggie's man and slam-dunking the ball over Andy Heller, who scrambled to get out of the way.

The subs finished the fourth quarter for the Patriots, and when the final buzzer sounded, the score was Jefferson 61 and Southeast 45. The Jefferson fans cheered, and the pep band played the school's fight song.

In the locker room, Coach Ford was all smiles.

"That's more like it," he said, "even though this was a weak team. With the exception of some of the bench players, you all played well and were into the game mentally."

"Man, we smoked 'em," Reggie said, peeling

his sweat-soaked jersey over his head. "We're rolling now!"

The team's scorebook went around and Brian was proud to see that he'd led all scorers with twenty-nine points. He'd made ten of fifteen long shots, swished both three-point shots he'd attempted, and had held Nelson Moore to only nine points and two rebounds. LaMont had scored in double figures with eighteen points, while Gary Simmons had led Southeast by scoring twenty-three points. And Clarence had pulled down an amazing total of twenty-two rebounds.

As the team celebrated with laughter and good-natured kidding, Brian just smiled and thought about how well Tyrone Russell's offensive moves to the basket had worked.

EIGHT

On Saturday morning over pancakes, Brian's aunt said, "Lordy, that was quite a ball game last night. Those boys from Southeast should've stayed home, don't ya think?"

Brian forked some pancakes and syrup into his mouth, then replied, "I reckon so, but we knew they were going to be pretty weak. Still, it sure was nice kicking somebody's butt for a change. And I'm glad we did it at home, too."

"Yes, and aren't your next three games away?" Brian's mom asked from the other side of the kitchen table. She was dressed and almost ready to go Christmas shopping.

Brian swallowed some pancakes and nodded. "Yeah, beginning with Lincoln North on Tuesday night." He ate some more pancakes, then smiled. "And after that, Christmas vacation. No games, no classes, just some practices, and—"

The telephone rang.

Aunt Margaret paused with her coffee cup halfway to her mouth. "Now who do you suppose that could be so early on a Saturday morning?" She stood and answered the nearby wall phone.

Brian looked up as his aunt's face wrinkled with puzzlement. "It's for you, Brian. Some newspaper guy." She handed him the telephone receiver.

He just shrugged and took the receiver. "Hello?"

"Brian, this is Gary Meyers of the Indianapolis *Gazette*. I'm a sportswriter, and I've followed your basketball career ever since your days up at Paintville High."

A pause followed, and Brian could only say, "Uh-huh."

"I'd like to do a story on you for tomorrow morning's sports section, if that's all right with you."

"A . . . a story? What kind of story?"

"You know, about your move to the big city and your impressions of things around here. And, of course, something about the basketball scene in Indianapolis. The whole interview shouldn't take more than half an hour. What do you say?"

Brian covered the receiver with his large hand. "The guy wants to interview me for the Sunday sports pages," he said with a growing smile. But then he recalled how uncomfortable he usually felt during interviews, and he frowned. "I don't know what to tell him."

Brian's mom put down her coffee cup. "Well, not everybody is asked for an interview. Besides, you're used to those things by now." His mom winked at him. "You can handle it, son, just like you handled those kids from Southeast last night."

Brian smiled and talked to Gary Meyers, who told him he would stop by the house at eleven o'clock. After the conversation, Brian hung up the phone and looked at his mom.

"Wow, an interview for the Sunday paper," he said.

For the rest of the morning, Brian alternated between looking out the front windows for any sign of the reporter to half watching cartoons on TV. Either way, his mind was already focusing on the upcoming interview, and he tried to imagine what kinds of questions he would be asked.

Halfway through an exciting episode of *Teenage Ninja Mutant Turtles*, the doorbell rang. Brian opened the front door and looked down at a smiling middle-aged man wearing wire-rimmed glasses who stood about five feet eight inches tall—a full foot shorter than Brian. The man was balding with wisps of brown hair and had a round pleasant face. Brian felt a nervousness in the pit of his stomach, but after the introductions he showed Gary Meyers into his Aunt Margaret's house and took the reporter's heavy winter coat to the hallway closet.

"Good morning," Brian's mom said, shaking

hands as she and Aunt Margaret stepped into the living room. "I'm Brian's mother, Mrs. Helen Davis, and this is Margaret Schmidt, Brian's aunt."

"Mornin'. I'm Gary Meyers of the *Gazette*. You both must be proud of Brian. Whether you realize it or not, he's one of the top high school basketball players in the entire state of Indiana."

Brian watched as his mom smiled and said, "Yes, we know." She stepped over to Brian and put her arm around his waist. "But he's still just my big baby," she added.

Brian felt himself blushing. "Mom . . ."

Gary Meyers chuckled, and then all of them sat down.

"I hope you don't mind if we listen," his mom said.

Meyers shook his head. "By all means, stay."

For the next half hour, Gary Meyers referred to a set of typed questions in his loose-leaf notebook and asked Brian all about his basketball playing days at rural Paintville High School, his tournament experience, and what he thought about the city of Indianapolis— especially its high school basketball. Meyers also asked for Brian's opinion about the other top high school centers in the city, namely, Oscar Brown at Westside High and particularly Dexter Cole at Lincoln North, since Brian and Cole were going to play against each other on Tuesday night.

Brian surprised himself and remained cool and calm during the entire interview. He was even enjoying himself. Perhaps it was because he was in familiar surroundings, or maybe it was his recent basketball success at Jefferson. But whatever the reason, he felt confident— even a bit cocky—as he answered Gary Meyers's questions. And to Brian's relief, his mom and aunt kept quiet for the whole half hour.

After Meyers left the house, Brian breathed deeply and asked, "Well, Mom, what do ya think? How'd I do?"

His mom reached up and kissed him on the cheek. "You did just fine, son. I'm even prouder of you now."

But his aunt said, "I just hope that fella can write as well as he can ask questions."

And Brian and his mom both laughed.

Sunday morning finally arrived, and Brian rushed downstairs in his pajamas and slippers, stepped onto the frigid front stoop to retrieve the Sunday *Gazette*, and quickly spread the bulky paper on the living-room carpet. When he finally found the sports section and glanced at it expectantly, he wished he hadn't.

"Lordy, it's so early," Aunt Margaret said, stifling a yawn. "Did they print your interview, Brian?"

"Let us have a look, son," his mom said.

Brian held up the newspaper with slightly trembling hands, and both his mom and his aunt leaned closer to look at it. A large photo of Brian dunking a ball accompanied the article. His mom read the story's headline aloud.

"'Brian Davis says Jefferson Patriots are tops,'" she said, reading the large print. "Nothing wrong with that." Then she read the story's subheadline. "'Six-eight star says Lincoln North and Dexter Cole are overrated.'" And as his mom looked at Brian, he noticed her mouth had dropped open. "Oh, my," she said.

"Why, you didn't say anything of the sort," Aunt Margaret said. "That's a lie!"

"I hope Dexter Cole and the fans at Lincoln North feel the same way," Brian say, "or I'm in big trouble."

"There must be some mistake, Brian."

"Mom," Brian said, nearly in tears, "this is awful."

The phone rang, and after Aunt Margaret answered it, she looked at Brian with a worried look on her face. "It's Coach Ford," she said, "and he sounds upset."

NINE

Before Coach Ford could say a word, Brian blurted out, "Coach, I didn't say that about Lincoln North."

"It's all right, Brian," said his coach calmy, managing even to chuckle. "I'm not upset with you, but with that Meyers guy. He's known for doing things like this. You're not the first one to be misquoted in one of his articles."

"What can we do about it?" Brian asked, starting to feel a little better.

"Well, I called the sports desk at the *Gazette*, and of course Meyers is unavailable for comment. But the damage is done, so even talking with the little weasel won't do much good. I just wanted to make sure you were okay."

Brian took a deep breath. "I guess I'll live," he

said. "I guess I should've kept my big mouth shut."

"Well, in basketball as in life, live and learn."

The coach then said he would speak with Mr. Rhodes to explain the situation to him, and talk about the article with the rest of the team at practice.

Brian spent the rest of Sunday ignoring his homework and worrying about the reaction to the article. Reggie and Tony dropped by after lunch to shoot some baskets and talk about it with him.

The next day, Brian was overwhelmed by the response from the students and the teachers. Most students said things like, "Way to go, Brian," and "That's how to tell off those Lincoln North brats." And all his teachers, even Miss Pinchot, mentioned how impressed they were that he had been the subject of a major sports article in the Sunday newspaper.

At practice, Coach Ford opened with a discussion of the article. "Sometimes these sportswriters can twist your words to fit the story they *want* to write," the coach said.

"And in this case," Coach Williams added, "it's obvious that this Meyers dude wants to build up a feud between us and Lincoln North." The heavyset coach looked at Brian and added, "And he'd like a feud between Brian and Dexter Cole to write about, too."

"But as far as I'm concerned," Coach Ford said, looking at all of the varsity players, "the case is closed. Just watch what you say to the press from now on, and that goes for all of you. Now, let's get ready for Lincoln North. They may be rated number seventeen in the state, but I know we can beat them."

"Hey, all right!" Tony shouted.

"Man, I've been looking forward to this for weeks," Reggie said.

Following a detailed scouting report about the Lincoln North Cardinals from B-team coach Pat Young, Brian and his teammates warmed up by running twenty-five laps around the floor and by doing their stretching exercises for ten minutes. Then, with the subs playing the role of the Lincoln North players, they spent over an hour reviewing North's offensive and defensive systems.

"And remember," Coach Ford said, "this Dexter Cole is six feet ten inches tall. And he likes to block shots, and is pretty good at it. So when you little guys shoot lay-ups, keep that in mind." The coach looked at Brian. "I suppose this is the first time you've played against a center taller than you, so watch out when you shoot your jumpers."

Halfway through the practice, Brian noticed that LaMont looked kind of sick. The lean black captain was breathing deeply and after a while began holding his stomach during the half-court scrimmages. A few moments later, Brian watched as Coach Williams walked over to LaMont and spoke with him for a while, and then felt his forehead. When LaMont nodded and ambled toward the locker room, Brian figured it was a case of the flu or a stomach virus.

As the last practice before Christmas vacation wound down, the players finished by running three-man fast breaks for fifteen minutes. With a few minutes remaining, Brian was returning to the lines at one end of the court when he heard a loud cry of pain from down near the far basket. He turned sharply. Jeff Burgess, his hands grasping his right knee, was rolling around on the court in a great deal of pain.

Both the coaches and the players raced to Jeff's side. When Brian arrived, he knew from just looking at how much pain the big football player was experiencing that the backup center's basketball season was most likely over.

"It popped," Jeff said though clenched teeth. "The damn knee just popped."

After Coach Williams helped Jeff hop downstairs to the locker room, Brian and the ten remaining players finished the fast-break drills—but with a lot less enthusiasm than before Jeff's injury.

In addition to its being the day of the big Lincoln North game, Tuesday was also the next-to-last day of school before Christmas vacation. All during the school day, the minds of the students seemed to be on a lot more than just basketball. Still, Brian was pleased when Reggie, Tony, and he discovered that enough students had signed up to fill four "spirit buses" for the trip across town to see that night's game.

"Man, Dexter Cole and his boys will look twice when they see all the Jefferson folk crowded into their gym," Reggie said.

"We oughta have as many fans there as Lincoln North," Tony added. "And we're going to need 'em to outyell all those spoiled brats up there."

"Bad fans?" Brian asked, walking to his last class of the day.

"Hey, man," said Reggie, "we're talking about kids with two VCRs, big cars to tool around in, the works. And those rich dudes like nothing more than to come out and yell at the poor boys from Jefferson." Reggie laughed.

"I guess the TV and newspaper folks will be there, too," Brian said.

"Sure," Tony said. "This is a big game."

"Yeah, but you just keep away from those sportwriters this time," Reggie said, breaking into a fit of high-pitched laughter, and then high-fiving Brian.

"I only wish LaMont felt better," Tony said. "I saw him during third period, and he looked bad."

"Hey, don't worry about my man LaMont," Reggie said. "He wouldn't miss a game as big as this, no way."

But as the varsity and B-team players assembled near the team bus after school, even including Jeff Burgess on crutches, Coach Ford gave them the bad news about LaMont. "He's running a fever of one hundred and two," the disappointed coach said, "and the school nurse told him to go home and rest."

"Well, we'll just have to beat Lincoln North without him. Right, guys?" the coach said.

"Right, right!" the team shouted.

"Yeah, let's do it!" Terry Hanson added, climbing onto the yellow school bus.

But even the shouts of enthusiasm couldn't hide the team's disappointment at losing LaMont.

The trip to Lincoln North's modern two-story educational complex took forty-five minutes through rush-hour traffic. The fairly new high school was on the outer edge of the city, and was actually considered a suburban school by most people. The student body was a mix of local white kids and inner city blacks who were bussed in.

After they stopped, Brian and the other varsity players followed the members of the B team off the bus and into Lincoln North's circular basketball arena, which seated five thousand fans. As Brian ducked through the gym's low doorway, he spotted the coaches and most of the players just ahead of him. They were reading a sheet of paper attached to an inside wall.

Tony, his stubbled face suddenly serious, stepped over to Brian and said, "Some jerk put copies of your newspaper interview all around their gym. I mean, it's everywhere."

Brian felt a cold dagger of anxiety in his stomach.

"Man, this is a bunch of crap," Reggie said.

"Worse than that," Coach Ford said, ripping one of the copies from the wall, "it's bush league. "That's Harlan Eckhorn, and he's been known to pull tricks like this newspaper interview thing everywhere he's coached. It's a trick to break your concentration on the game. So ignore it, guys, and just play."

"Coach," Cisco Vega shouted, returning with Alvin Woolridge from a quick tour of the circular gym's interior, "they even have copies near the bleachers so their fans can see 'em. There must be hundreds of copies around here."

"Yeah, but now there's a few less copies," Alvin said, holding up a handful and tearing them in half.

"All right, man," Terry Hanson said, high-fiving.

Brian was stunned, and he swallowed hard at the sudden realization that the fans at Lincoln North had decided *not* to forget about his published interview.

"Coach, look," Coach Williams said, pointing at a short, squat man with short-cropped gray hair and a bulging potbelly. The man was walking toward them. "There's their varsity coach."

The potbellied coach approached the group of players and coaches from Jefferson, and Brian thought Coach Ford was as upset as he had ever seen him.

"Welcome to Lincoln North High School, gentlemen," Eckhorn said, as if everything were normal. He glanced up at Brian for a moment, then extended his hand to Coach Ford. But the Jefferson coach just held up one of the copies.

"What's this crap, Eckhorn?"

Brian watched as Coach Eckhorn narrowed his eyes and glanced at the newspaper article, and then smiled somewhat knowingly. "Coach, I have nothing to do with the cheer blocks around here." His accent was vaguely southern. "They're the ones responsible for that."

"I'll bet," Coach Ford said, turning and marching toward the locker room. Brian and all the players hefted their equipment bags and followed. The Indiana High School Athletic Association will hear about this," Coach Ford called over his shoulder, "you can bet on *that.*"

"No need to get all riled up over it," Eckhorn said.

But when Brian and the others arrived in the large visitors' locker room, they found dozens of copies of the newspaper interview plastered all over the walls and lockers.

"Tear those things down," Coach Ford said.

And after both the B-team and varsity players finished removing the copies, Coach Ford said, "Don't let it upset you. While the B team is playing, just think about the job we have to do and focus your minds again."

"No problem, coach," several players said at once.

"Man, let's kick their butts for this," Reggie said.

The other players all shouted encouragement to one another. Brian began to feel a little better. Then, as the B team changed into their blue road uniforms and trotted onto the court for their preliminary game, Brian and the other varsity players decided to remain near their lockers. They figured that was safer than risking a confrontation in the gym with some angry Lincoln North fans.

"I saw a couple of TV vans parked near the gym. And you know the newspapers are going to be here, too," Tony said.

"Yeah, man, and we oughtta have some college recruiters on hand," Reggie said, spinning a ball on his index finger.

Brian just tried to focus on the upcoming game.

Later, as the B team was finishing its game and while Brian and the nine other healthy varsity players were putting on their blue road uniforms, Coaches Ford and Williams joined them for a review of the Lincoln North scouting report.

"All right," Coach Ford said, his composure back to normal again, "let's get our minds fixed on the game and everything we have to do here. First, remember what we said concerning Dexter Cole. He's six ten, and he blocks lots of shots."

"And," Coach Williams added, "you might be able to pump-fake him out of position as you're getting ready to shoot. He jumps at everything, so keep it in mind."

Cole's a senior, Brian, and he's an experienced offensive player," Coach Ford said. "You'll have to play a smart defensive game if we're going to hold him down."

Brian just nodded, trying to keep his butterflies under control.

Coach Ford continued, "As we discussed in practice, their other top scorer is Marty Shaw, a six-seven white kid who shoots a lot from the outside while Cole handles things under the hoop." The coach looked at Clarence. "Reed, Shaw is yours."

Brian watched as Clarence pulled his goggles down from on top of his head and nodded. "I'm looking forward to it."

Then the coaches discussed North's Bobby Pearson and Tommy Anders, two quick black guards who because of Cole and Shaw rarely got chances to shoot the ball, and the other forward, a defensive specialist named Wally Finn. And they reviewed Lincoln North's offense and defense before mentioning changes in the starting lineup: Reggie at forward for the ailing LaMont, and Alvin at guard.

Finally, Coach Ford said, "We can win without LaMont. Sure, we'd like to have him here, but since we don't, that means the rest of you will have to play just that much harder." The coach looked out over the players, and added in a stronger voice, "And, guys, I know you can do it."

"Yeah, all right!" said Cisco, the team's cheerleader.

"They think they're so hot, but let's show them something out there tonight," Terry said.

The B-team game ended with Lincoln North drubbing Jefferson by forty points, and after the court was cleared, Brian and the other Patriots shouted "Let's go!" and trotted out onto the floor amidst a chorus of loud boos from North's fans.

Almost immediately, Brian heard some cat-calls: "Hey, Davis, you stink!" "Davis, you're the one who's overrated!" "Go home, Davis!"

As they were shooting lay-ups, Brian tried not to listen. He hoped his mom and his aunt, who were sitting in the stands, weren't affected by all the abuse directed at him. He felt better when Reggie and several of the Patriot players patted him on the back.

"Just forget about 'em, man," Reggie said.

The Lincoln North Cardinals, dressed in flashy yellow-and-black warm-ups, dashed onto the floor amid an ear-shattering roar from their fans and their pep band and began to warm up. And fifteen minutes later, as the teams were being introduced to the sellout crowd, Brian nervously waited until it was his turn, and then with his legs feeling like rubber, he trotted out alone to join the other Jefferson starters already on the court. Once again he heard some catcalls—but this time from the Lincoln North players.

"Man, I'm going to eat you alive tonight," Dexter Cole shouted at Brian. Cole's lean black face was twisted with anger.

Six-foot-seven white forward Marty Shaw was shaking his balled fist at Brian as he said, "You don't look so tough to me, Davis."

Coach Ford yelled a protest at Harlan Eck-horn over on the North bench, but the potbel-lied coach just smiled back and spread his hands in a what-can-I-do gesture of frustration.

The opening tap was held amid an avalanche of cheers from both the North rooters and the smaller crowd of Jefferson fans. Brian and Dexter Cole just looked at each other, but neither spoke. The other players from both teams also kept quiet, but the tension in the air was crackling like electricity. The official tossed the ball up between the two young giants, and Dexter Cole leaped about three inches higher than Brian and won the tap.

Cole tapped the ball to forward Marty Shaw, who handed it to their small black playmaker Bobby Pearson to start the offense. Brian turned to run downcourt to play defense with the other Jefferson players, and almost immediately he felt Dexter Cole's elbow smacking away at his arms and chest. He knew then it was going to be a long and painful night.

Cole opened the scoring by slamming a lob pass from Pearson over Brian and into the hoop. On defense, Cole then blocked a lay-up attempt by Reggie and started a fast break that ended with a ten-foot jump shot by Marty Shaw, who raised his fist in triumph. Brian tried to make an offensive move to the basket against Cole and North's pressing man-to-man defense, but dribbled the ball off his foot. It was picked up by Tommy Anders, the other North guard. Anders fired a length-of-the-court pass to the streaking Dexter Cole, who once again slammed the ball through the hoop with a vengeance.

Coach Ford called for a time-out after three minutes. Lincoln North was leading 12 to 0. Dexter Cole had eight of their points and Marty

Shaw the remaining four. To make matters worse, Jefferson had managed to take only two shots at the basket, and one of them had been blocked by Cole.

"Man," Reggie said, slumping onto the bench.

Brian already felt bruised and battered, and it was just the start of the game.

TEN

"All right, guys," Coach Ford shouted over the cheers of the fans and the loud music of the Lincoln North band, "they were ready for us and really keyed up." He looked up at the scoreboard. "Okay, so it's twelve to nothing. Let's say for our sakes it's still zero to zero."

Brian, Reggie, and Clarence exchanged glances.

"Why not?" Coach Ford asked. "For whatever reason, North was gunning for us and we've taken their best shot. It's time to start over with ours!"

Brian looked at Reggie, who was nodding. "Sounds cool to me, man," the skinny guard said.

"Yeah, let's do it," redheaded Terry Hanson said.

And as the buzzer sounded ending the time-out, the Patriots huddled and shouted, "One, two, three, let's go!" Then, as they walked onto the court, Brian had to admit he felt better already. He was determined to fight back and decided to play hard for the remainder of the game, whatever the score.

Brian raised his hand in the corner and received a soft pass from Terry. As Cole jumped over to guard him, his face full of determination, Brian used a variety of Tyrone Russell's head, shoulder, and eye fakes to get the six-foot-ten-inch center to leap nearly a foot off the floor. Then Brian dribbled to the basket, jumped into the air, and dunked the ball.

The Jefferson fans cheered, and North went on offense.

Bobby Pearson quickly dribbled the ball into the halfcourt area, fired a chest pass to Marty Shaw on the right side of the basket, and set a pick on Brian in order to get Cole open for a shot. Brian saw Pearson's pick at the last moment and nearly trampled the little guard into the floor before stopping. Cole, free from Brian for a second, received a nice pass from Shaw and in one motion leaped into the air and swished a hook shot from fifteen feet away.

The Lincoln North fans roared, and Brian was determined to stop the hook shot the next time down the floor.

On offense again, Jefferson seemed more confident now. Terry Hanson, dribbling away from the superquick Tommy Anders, tossed a floating pass to Brian on the high post that just eluded Dexter Cole's fingers. Brian set up with the ball on the free-throw line and waited for Reggie to make a move on his man. Suddenly, Reggie faked toward Brian but then cut to the basket in a perfect back-door play. Brian fired a bullet pass to him, and he laid in the ball.

"Nice pass, man," Reggie said, high-fiving Brian as they ran back downcourt.

And for the remainder of the first quarter, Jefferson outscored the Lincoln North Cardinals. Despite ten points by Dexter Cole, four of them on sweeping hook shots, Jefferson trailed at the end of the first quarter by only eight, 21 to 13.

"Way to play guys," Coach Ford said. "They aren't so tough after all."

Jefferson continued its comeback in the second quarter. Brian missed two jumpers in a row, but the Patriots called plays for Reggie—who responded by swishing four long jumpers and one three pointer. And with two minutes remaining in the quarter, Jefferson was trailing by only two points, 30–28.

Lincoln North's coach called time.

"All right! Cisco Vega shouted, welcoming Brian and the other Jefferson starters back to the bench with high-fives all around.

Coach Ford substituted for the first time, giving Brian a rest after all the elbows he'd taken from Cole by sending Nick Vanos into the game. He also replaced Terry with Tony Zarella.

"Guys, even after that tough start, this game is still up for grabs," Coach Ford said.

And except for two hard-to-stop hook shots

by Dexter Cole over Nick and a free throw by Marty Shaw, the Jefferson subs finally held their own. Tony passed neatly to Clarence for a dunk shot one time down the floor, and Alvin hit a long jumper from the corner as time was running out. The score at the end of the first half was Lincoln North 35 and Jefferson 32.

In the locker room at half time, Brian flexed his arms and winced from the pain of all the bruises. Coach Ford, more excited then usual, praised the team for its comeback and urged it on.

But when the players took the court to start the third quarter, Brian noticed the look in Dexter Cole's eyes. It was as if he were telling Brian that the fun and games were over. And while Jefferson had trouble solving the sticky Lincoln North man-to-man defense, Dexter Cole and his teammates went wild for the first five minutes of the quarter, outscoring the Patriots by twelve to lead 49–34.

Cole opened the scoring with a sweeping hook shot over Brian's outstretched hands. Then, after Reggie missed a wide open lay-up down the middle, Bobby Pearson dribbled rapidly downcourt for North. Forcing Terry to lean one way while he tossed a pass the other way, Pearson found Marty Shaw unguarded in the right corner. Shaw then swished a fifteen-foot jumper. The scoring attack by Lincoln North continued with another hook shot and two slam dunks by Dexter Cole, and a long three point jump shot by Marty Shaw, on which he was fouled by Clarence twenty feet from the hoop.

Coach Ford called his second time-out.

Lincoln North always starts a quarter like gangbusters, scoring and running and jumping like crazy," the coach said. "Well, they've had their run for this quarter. Let's go out there and play tough defense, and look for good shots."

Back on the court, Brian and Reggie rallied strongly.

With three minutes to play in the third quarter and the score Lincoln North 49 and Jefferson 34, Brian and Reggie combined on three straight driving lay-ups. On two of the lay-ups, Cole committed fouls by slapping Reggie's arm and by crashing into Brian, and left the game for a rest. The score: North 49, Jefferson 40.

Cole's departure seemed to spark the Patriots. With George in for Terry and Reggie back at the guard position, the defense was quicker and better. And with Clarence grabbing every rebound that bounced his way, the Patriots were able to run some solid three-man fast breaks. Later, George passed to Reggie for an over-the-head lay-up and Alvin drew the defense to him by faking a three point shot and then fired a bullet pass to Reggie standing alone under the basket. Near the end of the quarter, Brian jab-stepped against Cole's substitute, then Brian leaped into the air and swished a long jumper from the left corner.

After three quarters: Lincoln North 52, Jefferson 49.

In the final quarter, the Patriots really showed how much they missed LaMont's leadership—as well as his twenty-points-a-game scoring average. While Reggie scored almost at will over little Bobby Pearson and the other North guards, the rest of the Jefferson players seemed fatigued—especially Brian, who was feeling the effects of battling Cole all evening.

With only two minutes to play in the game and North leading 70–64, Brian faked a drive to the basket against Dexter Cole. But the big North center didn't go for the jab-step fake. He leaped with Brian, whose legs felt as heavy as lead pipes, and blocked his usually untouchable jump shot. Cole tapped the ball to his teammate, Marty Shaw, who started a fast break downcourt.

Brian returned to the floor feeling stunned.

Dexter Cole just smiled.

With only a few seconds remaining, Bobby Pearson spotted Cole racing downcourt ahead of the tired Reggie and passed the ball. Brian was trailing the play. Cole took two giant steps to the hoop, brought the ball behind his head, and just before the final buzzer sounded he slam-dunked it through the basket.

The Lincoln North fans cheered, and Brian and his teammates walked from the court with their heads down.

The final score: Lincoln North 74, Jefferson 68.

And while several Lincoln North fans yelled insults at Brian as he was walking off the court, he was surprised when Dexter Cole stepped up behind him and told him, "Nice game, Davis." The rival centers high-fived each other, and despite the loss and the shock of having his newspaper interview plastered all over the gym, Brian felt better than he had earlier in the evening.

After showering, Brian glanced at the scorebook and noticed that Reggie had led the team in scoring with twenty-six points. Brian had scored only fourteen against the height and the elbows of Dexter Cole, while Clarence hit for thirteen and Alvin for eleven—including two long three pointers. Clarence again was impressive as a rebounder, hauling down fourteen. But once again, the bench hadn't produced many points, and Brian realized how much the team needed LaMont in order to be really successful.

Then, shaking his head in amazement, Brian saw that Dexter Cole had scored thirty-eight points and hauled in ten rebounds. He had also blocked several Jefferson shots. Marty Shaw finished with twenty-three points, mostly on long jumpers, but it was Dexter Cole who really hurt the Patriots in the game—and Brian now respected the six-ten center's ability even more.

As Brian waited to climb aboard the bus with the other players, he stepped on several discarded copies of his newspaper interview that were lying on the cold ground. He shook his head at the strangeness of the evening and vowed to get the team back to its winning ways following Christmas vacation.

After all, now they had five wins and two losses, and that wasn't good enough.

* * *

The following day at school was the last until after Christmas vacation, and both the students and the teachers were in a holiday mood. Even Brian and the other varsity players managed to get into the Christmas spirit, despite the loss to Lincoln North.

Part of the reason for the team's high spirits was the coverage the North game received in both the newspapers and on TV. And all of the various sportswriters were finally calling Jefferson one of the best teams in the state, and even mentioned Brian as being one of the top players.

At practice that afternoon, Coach Ford praised the players once for their effort against North, and laid out the practice schedule for the vacation period. Since no games were scheduled until school resumed on January third, the team was going to practice that day and the next, and then take four days off for Christmas. The coach said they would then start practicing hard again during the final week of the vacation.

"We have some tough games during the next two months," Coach Ford said, "and we'll have to work hard at correcting the mistakes we've made during the first part of the season."

LaMont was feeling better, and was practicing hard again. Jeff Burgess received the go-ahead from his doctor to resume basketball, and the big senior's courage impressed—and inspired—Brian.

At the next day's practice, after Brian and the rest of the players finally were able to sleep late,

the coaches reviewed the first seven games of
the season and discussed what the players
needed to work on. And Coach Ford mentioned
how especially proud he was of the way Brian
had worked so hard on his offensive moves with
Tyrone Russell.

Looking forward to the four-day Christmas
break from the Patriot's schedule, Brian, Reggie, and Tony rode a city bus to the downtown
community center for another session with
Tyrone Russell.

After the workout Brian and his two friends
helped Tyrone take about fifty young kids down
to the famous Soldiers and Sailors Monument at
the exact center of Indianapolis. At Christmas-
time, strings of lights hung from the top of the
180-foot-tall monument in a treelike formation,
and it was advertised as "the world's largest
Christmas tree." Everyone seemed to enjoy the
trip and the companionship, especially Brian.

ELEVEN

Christmas at Brian's aunt's house seemed even better than those he remembered at the country town of Paintville. And it was an especially happy occasion when he received several gifts from his father in Oklahoma—and his telephone call on Christmas morning.

It even snowed a little on Christmas Day, adding to the festive mood. And with a delicious roast turkey dinner prepared by his Aunt Margaret, Brian decided he was actually happy with his life in the big city. He was a city boy now, he reflected on Christmas Day, just like Reggie and Tony and his other teammates. He had adjusted to the hustle and bustle of city life, and, he realized with a chuckle, he could even fall asleep at night despite the noisy busses, cars, and trains.

And, he thought with a smile, he was a city basketball player, too.

The remainder of the school vacation was cold and snowy, and Brian fell into a routine of sleeping fairly late and going to basketball practice at the school gym. Coaches Ford and Williams worked the players hard after the four-day layoff to get them ready for their scheduled nine games in January.

Nick Vanos called in sick for the first two days of practice after Christmas. And Jeff Burgess was unable to run at full speed yet because of his bad knee, so Clarence had to play center during their scrimmages. But even with those minor problems, Brian enjoyed spending several hours each day doing nothing but playing basketball. It seemed like the life he thought professional basketball players led during the season. In his bedroom at night he looked at the many basketball posters on his wall and fantasized he was a professional player for the Indiana Pacers.

Brian, Reggie, and Tony also spent a few afternoons down at the community center with Tyrone and some other former high school stars. The fullcourt scrimmages in the musty old building allowed Brian to work on his offensive moves versus older and tougher players. Tyrone mentioned that he had set up a game with two members of the Indiana Pacers who often worked with Tyrone's kids.

"Me?" Brian asked. "Against NBA players?"

Tyrone laughed, and his round face brightened. "Sure, man, you can handle it. I've watched you get better every day down here. These professional dudes are going to be surprised what you can do."

On the last Saturday before school was scheduled to resume, Brian, Reggie, and Tony played on a team with Tyrone and another black former all-star. Their opponents were the Pacers' huge backup center, Artie Woodson, and six-five reserve guard Wiley Patterson, and three local former high school players.

"Man, look at the size of those NBA dudes," Reggie said, warming up for the scrimmage. "I'm glad *you're* the center Brian."

"I'll tell you one thing," Tony added, "I'm not driving down the middle today."

Brian and the others laughed, and the game began.

They were going to play until one of the teams reached thirty baskets, and after a coin flip, Brian's team started out on offense. Almost immediately Brian discovered what it was like going up against an NBA pivotman—it felt like leaning against a sweaty wall of flesh that kept pushing you away from the basket.

But during the first few times down the floor, Reggie managed to handle the ball against Wiley Patterson without much difficulty and passed the ball to Brian under the hoop. The first time Brian received the ball, he turned to face the basket for one of his accurate jump shots and Artie Woodson smacked the ball away. The second time Brian received a pass from Reggie, he kept his back toward the big seven-footer, tried several of Tyrone's fancy fakes with his head and shoulders, and then charged into Woodson's chest as the big center played smart defense and cut Brian off before he reached the hoop.

As the game progressed, Brian's team trailed by four or five baskets the entire time. Brian found himself relaxing more and actually having some success against Artie Woodson. Once, after receiving a pass from Tyrone, Brian found himself open on the right side of the basket about seventeen feet away. Seeing that Woodson was not coming out to guard him, Brian leaped into the air and calmly swished a long jumper.

The next two trips down the floor on offense, Reggie got the ball to Brian in almost the exact same position, and the results were the same: two swishes on long jump shots. On both shots, Artie Woodson didn't come out and guard Brian closely.

On the next trip up the court on offense, Reggie missed a lay-up and Tyrone rebounded, passing to Brian. Artie Woodson decided to play defense against Brian. Brian faced the two-hundred-eighty-pound center and looked him in the eyes.

"Come on, kid, shoot the ball," Woodson taunted.

Brian used several pump fakes with the basketball firmly grasped in both hands, and on the last fake he noticed Woodson's body balance shifted a little forward. At that moment, Brian took a giant step toward the baseline, dribbled twice, and slammed the ball down through the basket.

Wiley Patterson, Woodson's NBA teammate, laughed uncontrollably. "Artie, the kid faked you out, man."

"Nice move, baby," Tyrone said, high-fiving Brian as they trotted downcourt to play defense.

And for the rest of the scrimmage, Woodson, his professional pride bruised a little, played tougher against Brian. But Brian was ready for the challenge. Except for weighing about one hundred pounds less than Woodson and getting pushed around the court, Brian held his own on offense. He swished three more long jumpers, and even made another fancy drive to the basket, on which Woodson fouled him by smacking him on the side of the head.

"Sorry, kid," Woodson said as Brian tried to clear his brain after the blow.

The scrimmage finally ended with Woodson shoving his way under the hoop against Brian, where he received a lob pass from Wiley Patterson and muscled the ball toward the basket for a lay-up.

After the game Woodson walked over to Brian and shook his hand. "Kid, you're going to be something else once you get some more experience—and a few more pounds on your body. That's a real pretty shot you got there.

"See, man? You've got what it takes. And let me tell ya something, that Artie dude doesn't give out compliments too easily, you know?"

Brian felt his face blushing, and he shifted his feet self-consciously. "I guess I just had a good game today, that's all," he said.

And after the NBA players left the community center, Tyrone stepped over to Brian and smiled. "Man, today was your graduation from our little school of offensive moves," he said, high-fiving with Brian. "You're ready to go up against any dudes you gonna face on your schedule."

As Brian headed back for their neighborhood on the city's northeast side and his two friends, the biting cold wind and the blowing snow flurries didn't seem to bother Brian. Still glowing from the warm praise he'd received from Artie Woodson, he knew he was ready for the rest of the season.

TWELVE

Classes seemed especially long and boring on the Monday after the vacation. Brian could hardly wait for basketball practice to begin. Even seeing Lori Harper again after such a long layoff from school couldn't blunt his excitement about resuming the season.

At practice, B-team coach Pat Young arrived right after school let out for the day and began his scouting report on the Patriots' next opponent, the Western Central Blue Devils.

"Western Central," Coach Young began, "is basically a two-man team. They lost four starters from last year's Sectional champions, and this year's leading scorer is a five-foot-six-inch guard named Perry 'the Jet' Jeter, who's averaging thirty points a game."

"He's a real quick dude," said LaMont. "And he plays bigger than he is. He can jump."

"Yeah, man," added Alvin, "I've played against him for a few years. He likes to drive into the middle and then pull up quick for this little jump hook shot he uses. It's real hard to stop 'cause he holds the ball out away from his body and his hang time is something else."

"Their other top player is a junior center named Larry Fenwick," Coach Young continued. The coach adjusted his glasses and looked up at Brian. "He's a tall, skinny white kid with a real good shooting touch from about fifteen feet away. You can stop him, Brian, if you play up on him. He doesn't like to drive very much, and besides, he's kind of slow. And on defense he doesn't like to stray too far from the basket, so you should be able to shoot over him.

"Their other starters are all young kids who make lots of mistakes. Tommy Johnson and Barry Phinney at forward, and a slow white kid named Steve Sheridan at the other guard."

Following the encouraging scouting report, Brian and his teammates held their first organized practice session of the new year. LaMont was shaking-and-baking again, and Jeff Burgess was moving better after having undergone therapy for his battered right knee. Only Nick Vanos, who seemed sluggish and overweight, practiced poorly.

"Man," Reggie said in the locker room after practice, "I can't wait to face these Western Central dudes."

"Yeah, we need some big wins about now,"

Tony added. "We gotta make those pollsters rank us higher in the ratings. Especially with the Westside game coming up later in the month."

"Hey, that'll be Brian's chance to get back at Oscar Brown for what he did to him in the summer league," Reggie said, cackling with laughter. "I hear Oscar's told all his teammates at Westside about his three-sixty turn followed by that slam dunk over you while you were down in the lane."

Brian forced a smile. "Let's just worry about Western Central first," he said.

"Man," Alvin said as he walked past, "there ain't nothing to worry about."

Brian wasn't too sure following their last road game at Lincoln North.

As the bus carrying the Jefferson varsity and B-team basketball squads reached downtown Indianapolis en route to the Western Central game, snow was falling in blizzardlike conditions. A brisk wind was drifting the fast-falling snow over all the roads, and the driver was forced to edge the bus along the clogged city streets at about ten miles per hour.

They finally reached Western Central High School, another modern educational complex in a nearby suburb, forty-five minutes late. The B team was forced to dress quickly for their game. Brian and his varsity teammates watched the first half of the B-team's lopsided triumph over Western. Only four hundred people or so had been willing to battle the snowstorm to see the game between Brian's Jefferson Patriots (five wins and two losses) and the Western Central Blue Devils (two wins and four losses).

"I guess we're not much of a draw out here," Tony said, smiling as he looked out over the empty bleachers.

"Yeah, man," Reggie added, "not even a media star like Brian can bring out the crowd during a snowstorm."

Reggie and Tony laughed, but Brian just waited impatiently for the varsity game to begin. He hadn't felt this confident and eager to play since his freshman season at Paintville High.

After changing into their blue road uniforms and listening to Coach Ford and Coach Williams go over the Western Central scouting report, Brian and his teammates loosened up with stretching exercises in the locker room.

Finally the B teams finished their game. Brian and the other players left the locker room and trotted onto the court. Brian, could not remember playing in front of such a small crowd before, except perhaps for buddy basketball games during his grade-school days.

The quiet atmosphere in the large gymnasium created all the excitement of a dull after-school practice session. The cheering squads for both sides almost outnumbered the fans. Only a dozen or so Jefferson rooters were on hand.

After the playing of the National Anthem by a handful of Western Central band members and the introduction of the starting lineups, Brian and the other starters took the floor. They were followed by the Western Central Blue Devils, dressed in their blue-and-white home uniforms. Alvin immediately pointed to tiny Perry 'The Jet' Jeter as if to say, "He's mine," and Brian and the others quickly found the Western players they were supposed to guard.

Brian shook hands with six-seven Larry Fenwick. But Brian felt so ready to play that he could have been shaking hands with Artie Woodson. It didn't matter—he was psyched.

Then the official tossed the ball up between the two centers, and Brian easily outjumped Fenwick and tapped the ball to LaMont—who immediately had the ball stolen by little Perry Jeter. The several hundred Western fans on hand cheered, and Western started to run its offense.

"Let's hold on to the ball," Brian shouted as he ran back to play defense. "We can't give them anything."

Remembering the scouting report and the individual summaries of each Western player, Brian guarded Larry Fenwick but watched Perry Jeter out of the corner of his eye. When the tiny Western point guard faked Alvin out of position and raced down the middle of the foul lane, Brian waited for the proper moment before he left Fenwick unguarded and leaped at the driving Jeter.

Jeter saw Brian coming, and in a maneuver the little guard must have used often in order to survive in a game of giants, he spun around in a complete circle and tried to lay the ball into the basket. But Brian was prepared for the fancy move. He reached out with his long right arm and swatted the ball back toward the free-throw line, where Alvin picked it up.

Racing down the court toward the other basket, Alvin stopped at the opposite free-throw line and waited for his wing men to drive past him on the break, just as they did so often in practice. Brian, running easily away from Fenwick, yelled to Alvin, who passed him the ball on the right side of the foul lane. Brian received the pass, tóok two giant steps, and then slam-dunked the ball through the basket.

The small number of Jefferson fans cheered. "Way to go, Davis." Coach Ford yelled.

For the first six minutes of the opening quarter, the Jefferson Patriots played better than they had played so far that season. On defense, Brian and Clarence blocked four more shots between them, and Alvin learned how to stay with Jeter by giving the little guard some space to dribble in near the top of the key. On offense, Reggie and Alvin and the rest of the Jefferson starters soon discovered that, for this game at least, their strategy was going to be simple: give the ball to Brian and get out of the way.

With the slow Larry Fenwick guarding him, Brian quickly took command of the game. Shooting with an accuracy unheard of at most Indiana high school games, he scored Jefferson's next seven baskets—most of them fifteen feet from the basket.

By the end of the quarter, Brian had totaled twenty-two points, and Jefferson led 30–17.

Most of the Western Central points had come on spectacular drives by tiny Perry Jeter. But nothing could match Brian's outstanding scoring exhibition.

Even Larry Fenwick and his Western Central teammates, Brian noticed, were staring at him in awe as he jogged over to the Jefferson bench amidst a flurry of high-fives from his own teammates.

"What a quarter!" Cisco Vega shouted.

For all practical purposes, the game was over after the first quarter. Brian scored nine more points in the second period, for a school record thirty-one points at the half-time intermission, which found Jefferson leading 55–33. But Brian wasn't finished yet, and in the third quarter he noticed Fenwick obviously had been told by his coach to play closer to Brian and to stop him from shooting so many long jumpers. So Brian just used the many fakes and feints Tyrone Russell had taught him and drove repeatedly to the hoop for lay-ups and dunks for fifteen more points in the third quarter, giving him a total of 46 points already.

"Man, what a game," Reggie said to Brian after they returned to the bench at the end of the third period. "You can't miss!"

But with the score Jefferson 76 and Western Central 47 after three quarters, Coach Ford benched Brian and the other starters for the remainder of the game and let the subs play for the entire fourth quarter. And although Tony, George, Brad, Nick, Terry, and Cisco allowed Western to score 33 points in the final period, while managing to score only 11 themselves, nobody seemed to mind after Brian's spectacular shooting display in the first three quarters.

The final score: Jefferson 87, Western Central 80.

"My only regret," Coach Ford said in the locker room after the game, "is that more people didn't see Brain's performance tonight."

"Yeah!" Tony shouted.

"Way to go, Davis!" Clarence yelled. "Good job, man."

"And," Coach Ford continued, "somebody just told me that with his forty-six points, Brian was only four points away from tying the Jefferson High one-game scoring record."

Brian's teammates booed playfully, and Cisco said, "Coach, you should've put him back in."

The coach shrugged, and then continued. "The subs needed some playing time. Besides, he's going to have many more opportunities to break that record."

Then Coach Ford high-fived Brian, and the team cheered loudly.

THIRTEEN

The freshly fallen snow crunched under Brian's feet as he walked to school with Reggie and Tony the next day.

Mr. Rhodes greeted Brian at the front entrance with a wide smile and an enthusiastic handshake. While at the same time, some of the nearby students applauded and waved to Brian.

"Great job last night, son," Mr. Rhodes said, a broad grin creasing his round face. "All of us are proud of your great scoring performance. We know it'll just be a matter of time before you break the all-time school record for the most points in a single game."

When the principal walked away, Reggie cackled and shook his head. "Man, Brian, you are a gen-u-ine hero."

Brian just shrugged and waved to his two friends as he entered his homeroom.

At practice that afternoon and the next day, Brian and the Jefferson Patriots used their big win over Western Central to inspire them to work hard for Friday's game at Harry Truman High.

On Thursday, the coaches discussed the scouting report on the Truman Presidents. Coach Young mentioned that Truman's won-lost record was only one and seven this year, but that they were better than their record. Two of their losses were to Westside and Lincoln North, two of the state's best teams. And, Coach Young added, they had lost to North by only eight points.

"Their best overall player is a husky white forward named Lenny Bergman," the five-foot-seven coach said, adjusting his thick-rimmed glasses. "He can't jump a lick, but he's a fighter under the basket. He'll battle you for both offensive and defensive rebounds."

Coach Ford pointed at Clarence. "He's yours, big guy."

Clarence, who was cleaning the lenses of his protective goggles with his T-shirt, nodded. "The boy'll have to get past me first."

"And their only other big threat is a skinny black center named Otis Stripe," Coach Young continued.

"I know that dude," LaMont said, nodding his head. "He can't do too much on offense, but he can block a few shots on the 'D.' But Brian oughta be able to make him look sick out there. Man, the kid's only fifteen years old."

The coaches then mentioned how Truman's coach was in his first year as a head coach, and that he didn't seem to know much about the city's teams yet.

"They play a swarming type of zone defense," Coach Young told them, "but they also make many mistakes and leave people wide open for shots. And on offense they like to look for Stripe underneath the basket and for Bergman cutting off picks at the free-throw line."

As Brian and his teammates began the actual physical portion of Thursday afternoon's practice, Brian noticed a quiet confidence among the players. It wasn't the cockiness that led to a lopsided loss against Gary Tech earlier in the season, but a feeling that they had everything under control.

Later on Thursday, following practice and a quick supper at home, Brian traveled by bus with Reggie and Tony to a night scrimmage at the old community center downtown. The air outside was cold, and after walking from the bus stop bundled up like Eskimos, even the smelly, warm interior of the dilapidated center seemed inviting.

As Brian entered the community center, Tyrone Russell stopped playing and greeted him with a broad smile.

"Man, forty-six big points!" Tyrone said, laughing. "You know, my playing career was cut short because of what happened at college." Brian was taking off his heavy parka when he stopped and noticed a thoughtful expression pass over Tyrone's round, happy face. "But now, with you doing so well, man, it's like . . . well, it's almost like I'm playing again, you know."

Brian really didn't know what to say, so he just high-fived Tyrone, who smiled and rejoined his game on the warped community-center court. But he had no doubt that Tyrone's comments came from the heart, and he was glad he was able to help the former Jefferson all-star feel like part of the team again.

After an hour or so of fullcourt pickup games, Brian looked up and saw that Wiley Patterson, the six-five black guard for the Indiana Pacers, had just entered the building and was being mobbed by a dozen or so little kids. Tyrone, Brian, and the others greeted the lean professional player, who warmed up for ten minutes at one of the baskets before he looked at Brian and motioned for him to join him.

"Hey, man, let's go one-on-one," Patterson said. "For fun."

"Me?" Brian said rather stupidly.

Patterson chuckled. "Sure, anybody who can score forty-six points in a high school game can play me or anybody else one on one." He tossed the ball he was dribbling to Brian. "Your ball out. We play to twenty."

Brian just nodded and got into position.

As Tyrone, Reggie, Tony, and all the others in the community center gathered around to watch the matchup, Brian dribbled the ball out to the top of the key and turned to face Wiley Patterson. He couldn't believe he was actually about to go one on one with one of the country's three hundred professional basketball players.

Patterson crouched in a defensive position as if Brian were going to drive to the basket. Instead, Brian jab-stepped toward the basket, getting Patterson back on his heels, then lofted a twenty-foot jumper. The ball swished through the basket and barely rippled the cords.

Patterson smiled and looked at Brian, then retrieved the ball and began to back in toward the hoop. Brian waited until the six-five guard's back made a little contact against Brian's forearm, and then waited for Patterson to make his move. The pro guard turned quickly and began a fallaway jump shot from about fifteen feet away. But Brian was already airborne, his long arms extended to their fullest, and he slapped the shot away just as it left Patterson's hands. Brian grabbed the ball and dribbled to the top of the key to begin his offensive moves.

The kids cheered; Patterson looked shocked.

And for the next ten minutes, Brian dominated Wiley Patterson in a manner neither of them had expected. Brian swished all but one of his long jumpers, used a few of Tyrone's fakes to get Patterson out of position, and finally won the one-on-one match twenty baskets to fifteen.

Afterward, a sweaty Wiley Patterson shook Brian's hand. "Man, you've come a long way since I first saw you down here. You're going to be a great player."

And with the words of the Indiana Pacers' guard warming him more than his heavy parka ever would, Brian trudged back home with

Reggie and Tony through the chilly darkness and looked forward to the next day's game at Truman High.

After all, Brian thought, *I'm on a roll now.*

FOURTEEN

Harry Truman High was a large school on the northwest side of the city, and Brian learned from Reggie and Tony that the school's sports teams hadn't had much success during the past few years, especially their basketball teams.

"But, man, we better kick butts tonight," Reggie said as they rode through the darkened city in the drafty school bus, "because we got some tough games coming up."

"Yeah," Tony added, "we can't let these scrub teams catch us on an off night."

Brian smiled. "Well, I guess we just can't have any off nights," he said, looking at his two friends.

When the team bus dropped them off at the large Truman High gym, Brian and the other varsity players let the B team dress and trot

onto the court before they took over the locker
room themselves. After selecting a locker for
himself, Brian joined his teammates in the large
Friday night crowd and watched as the Jefferson B team demolished Truman's B team in the
first half of their game, 43–21. As the first half
ended, Tony nudged Brian and pointed at the
two different TV minicam crews arriving inside
the gym.

"What are they here for?" Tony asked.

"Man, I bet they're here to watch our country-
boy center score some points," Reggie said,
flashing a toothy smile.

"I reckon they're just here to tape some
highlights for the eleven o'clock sports news,"
Brian said, walked toward the locker room with
the rest of the Jefferson varsity players. "You
know, they always have some games on tape to
show on Tuesdays and Fridays."

"Naw," Cisco Vega said, joining Brian, Reggie,
and Tony. "Those guys are here to watch you
score, man. They sure aren't here to watch
Truman."

"That's for sure," LaMont said, walking up to
them.

And all the players, including Brian, laughed
as they entered the locker room to change into
their blue away uniforms.

The B-team game ended with Jefferson winning 70–37. The varsity ran onto the floor amidst
a round of applause from the cheerleaders and
a large Jefferson cheer block, including Brian's
mom and aunt.

At the end of the warm-up period, Brian

looked around at the Truman Presidents, dressed in their home white uniforms and orange warm-up suits, and felt his adrenaline beginning to surge. The buzzer sounded, indicating the beginning of the game was only moments away.

Once the starting lineups for both teams were introduced to the enthusiastic crowd, Brian and the usual starting five, with Terry back at guard, huddled around Coach Ford.

"Remember," the coach said over the noise of the cheerleading squads from both schools, "these guys lost to Lincoln North by only eight points. And they play a swarming type of zone defense. Keep your cool on offense, and somebody should be open for a good shot. And on defense, play tough man-to-man."

Coach Ford stuck out his hand, and Brian and the others slapped theirs on top of it, after which they all said, "Let's go!" and walked out for the opening jump ball.

"You've been hot lately," redheaded Terry Hanson said to Brian as they lined up for the tap play, "so I'll be looking for you a lot. Get open and I'll get you the ball."

Brian nodded, and then turned to face the skinny six-foot-nine-inch Truman center, Otis Stripe. The young black sophomore shook hands with Brian, and the official tossed up the basketball.

Brian won the jump and tapped the ball to LaMont. He passed it to Terry, who dribbled downcourt to set up the offense. But as Brian turned to run after his teammates, he noticed

that Otis Stripe was still standing in the midcourt jump-ball circle, as inexperienced players
sometimes did.

Brian took advantage of Stripe's mistake and
raced toward the basket, his left hand raised.
"Hey!" he called to Hanson.

Terry fired a bullet pass to Brian at the top of
the key, and Brian took two long steps, brought
the ball over his head, and slammed it down
through the hoop for a rim-rattling dunk.

The Jefferson fans cheered. Otis Stripe grimaced.

From the outset, Brian knew this game was
going to be something special. He felt like a
finely tuned machine running with all its parts
functioning perfectly. On defense, he spent the
entire first quarter smothering poor Otis Stripe
with his long arms. And on two occasions, he
even took the basketball right out of the sophomore's hands and started Jefferson fast
breaks. The other Jefferson starters, especially
Reggie, who made four steals in the quarter,
also stopped the disorganized Truman offense
in its tracks.

On offense, Jefferson looked for Brian for the
second game in a row. And for the second
straight game, Brian had himself a perfect first
quarter.

Once he used his shake-and-bake moves to
leave Stripe in the dust and slam-dunked another basket through the hoop.

Later, he faked the drive and pulled up for a
fifteen-foot jumper, which swished through the
net.

On yet another drive, Brian suddenly found himself being guarded by *three* Truman players at the same time. He held the ball over his head until he finally spotted Reggie open near the free-throw line and passed it to him. The very quick Truman defenders leaped over to Reggie, leaving Brian free for a quick cut to the basket. Reggie fired an overhead pass to Brian for an easy give-and-go lay-up.

As the first quarter wound down to its final few seconds, Brian found himself being shoved out of the lane by both Otis Stripe and husky forward Lenny Bergman. He raised his hand for a pass and received a perfect lob from Terry. Brian grabbed the ball on the right side of the basket, pump-faked once with the basketball, and watched as both Bergman and Otis Stripe leaped as high as they could in what looked like a Harlem Globetrotters' trick play of some kind. Brian then leaped as the two defenders were returning to the floor and calmly swished a long jumper just before the quarter ended with the score Jefferson 36, Truman 12. Brian had scored twenty of his team's points.

"Way to go, Davis," Coach Ford said, patting him on the back.

"Nice passes, Terry," Brian said, high-fiving the redheaded guard. "Great defense out there, guys."

While the fans buzzed about Brian's incredible performance, Coach Ford substituted Nick for Brian, George for LaMont, and Alvin for Terry to start the second quarter. As Brian sat on the bench with a towel, his adrenaline still

pumping through his body, he looked over at the
dejected Truman players and could see defeat
in their faces.

The second quarter was a bit tighter, thanks
to some silly plays by the Jefferson subs. Nick,
huffing and puffing and obviously out of condition, was no match for tall Otis Stripe, who now
that Brian was out of the game seemed to feel
free to whirl to the hoop for several easy
lay-ups. Chunky Lenny Bergman muscled his
way for several baskets following rebounds
against George Ross, who committed three
fouls trying to keep the big Truman forward
away from the backboards. And the guards,
Alvin and later Cisco and Tony, shot six times
without hitting a basket, and even threw away
the ball several times trying to pass it to Nick.

Brian returned to the game later in the second quarter with Jefferson still holding a big
lead, 50–29. He immediately reminded Truman
he was back by ending the first half with three
straight swishes of long jump shots, the final
one just as the half-time buzzer sounded.

The score at half time: Jefferson 57, Truman
31.

In the locker room, Coach Ford didn't even
talk to the team, and Coach Williams just told
them to rest a little and drink some Gatorade.
And as the second half began, Brian noticed that
the TV cameras were trained on him as he
sauntered out to midcourt to open the half.

"Hey, man," Reggie said, elbowing Brian playfully, "smile for your adoring television audi-

ence." The skinny guard laughed his usual high-pitched cackle.

The second half started much the same way as the first, with Brian receiving as many passes as his teammates could get to him. In just the first five minutes of the third quarter, he swished four out of six shot attempts, as well as six of seven free throws. Coach Ford replaced him with Nick Vanos, and Brian rested on the bench for the remainder of the quarter.

After the third period ended with Jefferson leading 77 to 49, Brian huddled around Coach Ford with the rest of the Jefferson varsity and watched as the coach looked up at him.

"Davis, Coach Williams tells me you've got forty points already tonight and that you're only eleven away from breaking the school's single-game scoring record. We don't usually think much about individual point totals and statistics, but if you want, I'll keep you in there for a chance at the record."

"Do it, man," Reggie said, his eyes aglow with excitement.

"Yeah, a school record," Cisco Vega said, looking up at Brian. "I mean, that's something special."

Brian looked over at Coach Williams, who was stroking his black-and-silver goatee. "It's up to you, man," the heavyset assistant coach said. "Just remember, you may never get this close to the record again."

Brian smiled. "Okay, let's go for it," he said.

And as his teammates high-fived him, Brian

looked at the TV cameras and noticed they were pointing at him again.

The final period opened with Brian a little cold from having sat on the bench during the latter part of the third quarter. He shot four jumpers over Otis Stripe during the first several minutes of the period, and made only one. The others were way off target, and Brian wondered if he was going to regain his shooting touch in time to break the record.

With five minutes to go and Jefferson leading by almost thirty points, Brian received a pass from Alvin down under the basket. He pump-faked once, then laid the ball into the basket— but was accidentally slapped in the face by Otis Stripe. Brian felt a stab of pain in his left eye and brought his hands up to his face.

"You all right, man?" Otis stripe asked, sincerely concerned.

Brian nodded at the tall sophomore center, and then tried to focus on the basket for his free throw. His eye was watering like a faucet, and Brian heard Coach Ford asking him if he could continue.

Bouncing the ball prior to his free throw, Brian looked at the coach and said, "No problem, coach." He smiled, and then swished the free throw.

During the next three and a half minutes, Brian had trouble receiving passes from his teammates. The Truman Presidents double- and triple-teamed him every time he ran downcourt. With twenty seconds remaining, Brian had forty-seven points, but Truman had the basket-ball in their halfcourt area.

As Lenny Bergman, Truman's beefy forward, dribbled toward the basket and then passed up an open shot in order to waste time so Brian couldn't have any more shots, Reggie under-stood what was happening. The skinny guard waited until just the right moment and stepped between Bergman and the inexperienced guard to whom he was about to pass the ball.

The Jefferson fans rose and cheered.

Brian took off downcourt, leaving Truman's reserve center wondering where he had gone.

As the clock ticked away the seconds, Reggie led Brian perfectly with a long pass that Brian caught while racing at top speed toward the hoop. Brian turned and scored an unguarded lay-up.

Brian had forty-nine points. Seven seconds remained.

"Press 'em!" Coach Williams shouted from the bench.

"Let's get in their faces!" Reggie yelled to the Jefferson players on the court.

Lenny Bergman arrived to inbound the ball, but took his time as the seconds continued to tick away.

The clock read 0:07, 0:06, 0:05.

Then, just before the five seconds Bergman had to throw the ball inbounds elapsed, Brian noticed that only Truman's reserve center was open. The remaining players all were being closely guarded by Brian's teammates.

The clock ticked away: 0:04, 0:03.

Brian figured the only place Bergman could toss the inbounds pass was to the center, who was standing thirty feet from the basket. Just as Bergman pulled back his arm and fired the pass, Brian leaped and intercepted it before it even reached the stunned center.

In the same motion, Brian turned and lofted a thirty-foot desperation heave at the basket.

The basketball floated toward the hoop, smacked against the glass backboard, and swished back down through the cords as the buzzer sounded.

Brian's teammates raised their arms in cele- bration, and then mobbed him. Coach Ford, smiling from ear to ear, joined in, high-fiving Brian.

The final score: Jefferson 94, Truman 63.

And Brian had the new school scoring record.

The TV cameras closed in for the happy scene, as most of the Patriots finished slapping high-fives with their star center and headed for the locker room. Brian hung back with LaMont, Reggie, Clarence, Tony, and Coach Ford as a middle-aged TV sports reporter stepped up to him.

"Brian Davis, I'm Jim Washburn of WAGX- TV," he shouted over the postgame confusion. "I'd like to talk with you about your terrific win tonight."

Brian paused to look at the coach, who smiled and nodded his approval.

"Sure, Mr. Washburn," Brian said confidently. "But first I want to say that I'm real proud to be part of a great team like the Jefferson Patriots."

"All right, Davis! Jefferson all the way!" Reggie and the other boys cheered, their fists raised high in a victory salute.

Star center BRIAN DAVIS has to face some tough players both on and off the court to lead the Jefferson Patriots to victory in the next exciting book:

HOOPS #3: BACKBOARD BATTLE

INTRODUCING

★HEROES★
INC

EXCITING NEW SERIES
THAT ARE ADVENTURES IN
IMAGINATION!

BLITZ